dust storm? Polrus asked without much hope. Krusk jogged through the company, stoically ignoring the pain and frustration of those around him. Stopping in front of the captain, he gave his report.

"They're coming, Captain," he growled. He had his bow in his hands, strung. "An hour back at this pace, maybe less."

Tahrain cursed. "So they've caught us. . . ."

**From the creators of the
greatest roleplaying game ever
come tales of heroes, monsters, and magic!**

By T.H. Lain

CITY OF FIRE

T.H. Lain

CITY OF FIRE

Distributed in the United States by Holtzbrinck Publishing.
Distributed in Canada by Fenn Ltd.

Distributed to the hobby, toy, and comic trade in the United States and Canada by
regional distributors.

Distributed worldwide by Wizards of the Coast, Inc. and regional distributors.

Made in the U.S.A.

Cover art by Todd Lockwood
First Printing: September 2002
Library of Congress Catalog Card Number: 2002110751

9 8 7 6 5 4 3 2 1

US ISBN: 0-7869-2854-9
UK ISBN: 0-7869-2855-7
620-88250-001-EN

U.S., CANADA,
ASIA, PACIFIC, & LATIN AMERICA
Wizards of the Coast, Inc.
P.O. Box 707
Renton, WA 98057-0707
+1-800-324-6496

EUROPEAN HEADQUARTERS
Wizards of the Coast, Belgium
P.B. 2031
2600 Berchem
Belgium
+32-70-23-32-77

Visit our web site at **www.wizards.com**

To Jill

whose patience, confidence,

and support made this possible.

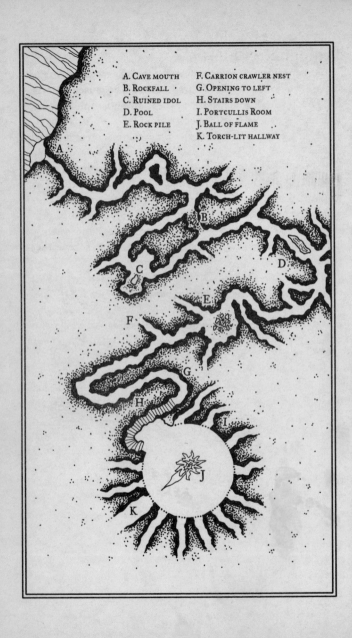

A. Cave mouth
B. Rockfall
C. Ruined idol
D. Pool
E. Rock pile
F. Carrion crawler nest
G. Opening to left
H. Stairs down
I. Portcullis Room
J. Ball of flame
K. Torch-lit hallway

Prologue... The city burned.

Tahrain wiped his brow and peered into the darkness, straining his eyes to the north. Nothing but sand, he mused bitterly, but he knew that somewhere, perhaps a hundred miles away, Kalpesh burned—if it still stood at all.

And yet he, the city's guard captain and Protector of the Opal Throne, abandoned Kalpesh's defense and fled into the desert on a vital mission that looked more hopeless every hour. For easily the twentieth time that day, his brown, callused hand found its way inside his light chain shirt to the oilskin packet against his right breast. He looked up and scanned his eyes over the faces of the few men and women who now lay in small clumps silently around him. They did not notice as his fingers found the leather thong and checked its secure knot.

Shaking himself out of his reverie, Tahrain turned again to his remaining soldiers. His most loyal troopers, twenty of Kalpesh's finest, followed him into the desert to die without any explanation. Only one man knew Tahrain's true mission in the wastes, and he wasn't even a man by most civilized folk's standards. Most called him "brute" at best, but Tahrain knew differently. He looked for this brute among his exhausted soldiers.

The captain's eyes found the person they sought. Every man and woman in their company lay splayed out under the black desert sky, hoping to forget hunger and thirst in the short respite a fitful slumber offered. Everyone but himself, he thought, and this one person. The brute stood alone, on the other side of their makeshift camp, looking northward into the desert night. When Tahrain had found him, years ago, the creature was alone, dressed in tatters, and nearly dead from numerous wounds. Even now his armor looked as if someone cobbled it together from three different-sized suits, and his weapon, a brutal greataxe, was stained and notched, and appeared as if its haft might break on the very next swing.

If this soldier's kit looked mismatched and ugly, it was simply a reflection of the wearer. Long-armed and grey-skinned, he appeared to be made of disparate parts himself. His body refused to blend together in the normal way, as if his bulging eyes and jutting chin wanted to escape the confines of his face. His hair looked as if it had been hacked at with a knife, and it was obvious his swollen arms and legs had been, once. He wore no boots on his oversized feet but only light sandals, held on with makeshift straps.

Tahrain rose painfully and quietly. He did not want to wake any of the soldiers that managed to find sleep. Picking his way carefully around the huddled clumps, he moved across the camp.

The man who turned to watch his captain approach was a half-orc. Born almost certainly out of violence, forced to live hard and doomed to die violently, half-orcs looked as if their own bodies struggled to free their separate halves from each other. This struggle, Tahrain had heard, usually spilled out into the world, making half-orcs unpopular in civilized lands. Certainly, when Tahrain brought this one to the city and insisted he be nursed back to health, there had been more than a few who'd wondered (privately or aloud), "Why bother?"

Tahrain hoped to answer that question soon.

"Krusk?" he whispered.

The bulging eyes stared at Tahrain. One fang protruded from the half-orc's lower jaw up over his scarred, thin upper lip. His face twisted into what others might interpret as a snarl. The captain knew it for a smile, as close to one as Krusk could get. That didn't mean the half-orc was happy, though. Krusk was seldom happy.

"They're closer," he growled.

Tahrain nodded. He'd guessed as much. He cursed inventively at his pursuers, but only briefly. Krusk waited, as stoically as ever, for the captain to speak.

"How close?"

"Eight hours. Maybe nine," Krusk grumbled in his deep, gravelly voice.

Tahrain didn't know how the half-orc had divined this information, but he knew it was accurate. Among his soldiers he had many rangers—he was skilled in the lore of the wilderness himself—but Krusk had something more. If the half-orc said their pursuers were a day's ride from catching them, the captain believed him.

Tahrain shook his head and sighed, "We won't make it, will we?"

The half-orc simply stared at him, then looked away and shrugged.

"They're weak," he said eventually.

Krusk seldom spoke and knew little of tact. The half-orc probably didn't even think calling the best soldiers of Kalpesh "weak" was an insult.

"But you're not," Tahrain finally said. "You could make it? Alone?"

Again the half-orc shrugged. He loomed almost a full head over the tall captain, but somehow the shrug made Tahrain think of a child who had something to say he knew his parent wouldn't like.

"What is it, Krusk?" he asked gently.

Looking off into the darkness, back toward the pursuers they both feared, Krusk shifted his weight, digging holes in the sand.

"I won't go," he said after a long pause. "You saved my life."

"As you've saved mine since," Tahrain said. "If I were a man to keep score of such things, we'd be even. But we don't keep score like that, do we, Krusk?"

The half-orc didn't look back, and Tahrain didn't push. Arguing with Krusk was like arguing with the desert wind.

"Let's get to our lesson, shall we?"

The captain took a few labored strides out into the darkness, farther from the camp, and Krusk followed. Tahrain walked until the two put a small dune between themselves and the other soldiers. He sat down heavily in the sand, with Krusk crouching before him. If the half-orc craned his neck, he could still see the exhausted soldiers. They'd done this for the past six nights, but Tahrain feared this would be the last time.

Drawing the leather packet from inside his mail shirt, the captain opened it slowly. He showed Krusk the brittle papers inside and talked him through the contents of each one, and made Krusk repeat, in a voice as low as the half-orc could manage, everything Tahrain told him. Krusk couldn't read, but his memory was perfect. When they finished, Tahrain went over everything again. They started a third iteration but the half-orc put a hand on the captain's shoulder. Only then did Tahrain realize he was drifting off, still talking though nearly asleep.

He shook himself and said, "I need sleep…" But as Krusk stood Tahrain grabbed his thick wrist. "Wait! There's one more thing. Whether we make it to the canyon or not, Krusk, this has to get there, and beyond. It has to be kept from the hands of those who even now burn Kalpesh for it, and it has to make its way into the right hands. Even more than the protection of the city, this has been my sworn and secret duty, as it was my mother's before me and her father's before her. Every Protector of the Opal Throne swears to protect this beyond the lives of his soldiers and even the life of the city itself."

Tahrain blinked, for a moment fully awake. He locked his dark eyes on the half-orc's mismatched pupils, trying to will the barbarian to understand.

"I fear, Krusk… I fear my city has been consumed in flames by now," he said, "but that doesn't change a thing. Those who came to Kalpesh came for this. You can't let them take it."

He pushed the packet into Krusk's hands. Taken aback, the half-orc fumbled the packet, then tried to hand it back to his captain. A small, golden disk among the papers shimmered in the starlight. Tahrain pressed the half-orc's hands between his own, tucking the disk back into the pouch.

"No. This goes beyond everything else. There's something I haven't told you."

The half-orc pulled the packet back, but still he hesitated. He waited patiently, though, for his friend to continue.

"The secrets I protect lead to a treasure beyond either of our imagining. If that was all, I would have gladly given it up to save Kalpesh, but the treasure is secondary. These secrets are secrets of

4

power. This disk is the key to an empire beyond this world."

Tahrain paused, the adrenaline fueling his tired limbs was spent. The half-orc stared at Tahrain with a look that said he was hearing everything and storing it away, even if he didn't understand.

"It isn't just a matter of getting this somewhere safe, or keeping it from those who desire it," the captain continued. "The attack against Kalpesh is proof that someone else knows about this." Tahrain wiped his brow and looked down. The disk was still partially visible and he fixed his gaze on it. "I don't know everything there is to know about it. I've told you everything I do know, these last few nights. I know that the time has come for someone to seal the gate and destroy the key. I'm sorry, but it has to be you."

The captain looked toward the meager camp, but his soldiers hadn't stirred.

"I'm giving this to you so you can finish a job that began centuries ago. I've made you learn every part of it in case we can't make it to the canyon. You've got to get away and carry this knowledge somewhere safe. Find people you can trust to help you, and then do the things I taught you.

"We can't all make it, Krusk," he whispered. "Unless a miracle occurs, you're the only one."

"No. You're the captain. You will make it," Krusk said, as if the strength of his words could make them true, but Tahrain shook his head and smiled sadly.

"I won't. I can't leave them—" he waved his hand at the sleeping guardsmen—"Fortune is against me, but my whole life has been dedicated to this task. Through you, I can fulfill it."

Tahrain put his hand on the packet Krusk still held. He pressed it against the half-orc's chest. Reluctantly, Krusk tucked it away inside his armor.

When Tahrain finally threw himself down amid his soldiers, his eyes still found Krusk standing alone near the edge of the camp, the half-orc's face turned toward the darkened desert.

"Captain! Look!" one of the soldiers on point called out, drawing the attention of everyone with any attention to spare.

She waved her arms and gestured toward the horizon. In the light of the new morning, Tahrain squinted ahead and saw the unmistakable outline of hills.

Still far off in the distance, but within sight, he thought as he felt a grim strength renew itself in his limbs. There is hope. The canyon is safety. If we can reach it, we'll stand a chance.

A cry from the rear of the company interrupted Tahrain's hopeful thoughts. The warning came from Krusk. Tahrain squinted back toward the source of the sound and felt his empty stomach sink. A cloud of swirling sand broke the evenness of the horizon behind them.

"Dust storm?" Polrus asked without much hope.

Krusk jogged through the company, stoically ignoring the pain and frustration of those around him. Stopping in front of the captain, he gave his report.

"They're coming, Captain," he growled. He had his bow in his hands, strung. "An hour back at this pace, maybe less."

Tahrain cursed. "So they've caught us. We can't reach the canyon ahead of them. Now's the time."

He looked pointedly at Krusk. The half-orc ignored him but Polrus opened his mouth to ask a question.

Krusk interrupted, "Can you run?"

Polrus blinked, then shut his mouth.

A sneer came to his lips but Krusk leaned in and growled, "Run or die, human. Your choice."

The challenge was all the lieutenant needed.

"We can run," Polrus said loudly.

The soldiers around him looked up, startled. He licked his dry, cracked lips.

"We can run, half-breed," he said even louder, shrugging out of his pack and throwing its useless weight to the ground.

Most of the soldiers followed their lieutenant's lead, abandoning everything they couldn't use in a fight.

"Everyone! Get in close," Tahrain called.

The soldiers kept moving forward, but clustered around their captain. They were tired, sore, and thirsty, but they hadn't given up yet. Tahrain blinked in the sunlight. He was proud of them, and he wished he hadn't doomed them all.

"The canyon's ahead," Tahrain called. "It's not close, but if we can make it there, we can use the cover of the rocks to punish them for what they did to our city." It wasn't a rallying cry so much as a statement of hope. "They're close behind. I want everyone to jog, double time, and drain your waterskins if you've anything left."

Some looked at the captain with confusion, but most understood. Water would do them no good if they died before they could drink it.

"Keep them and your weapons, drop everything else. If you can't run," the captain continued, already panting, "don't try." His face darkened as he said what needed to be said, "And don't stop for anyone. If you can't keep up, stop where you are and find cover. Slow them down. Die with honor."

As the captain ran, he looked around and saw grim determination on the faces of men and women he'd known for years. His lieutenant, Polrus, jogged by his side, and when their eyes met, he simply nodded. They trusted him, he knew, and they were content in their duty.

Then they heard the howls.

At first, the sound was like wind raking across the dunes. Then the sound came like dogs baying in a hunt. That would have been frightening enough, but there was something about the howls that didn't seem like the wind, or like dogs, but like a language. The howls had words in them, foul, inhuman words crying out behind the exhausted soldiers.

Soldiers started to run, not jog. Bursts of adrenaline carried a few men and women past the front of the company.

When the captain noticed their discipline breaking, he called out to Polrus, "Keep everyone together! No running—double-time, that's all!"

The captain panted. The lieutenant stumbled but kept up the pace as he moved toward those who seemed on the edge of panic. He couldn't get to them all, but most started to slow, to maintain a steady pace. Those that didn't slow, the company passed in minutes, gasping, struggling on the ground, trying to stand.

"Fight," the half-orc said as he passed the fallen. "Die with honor."

Before long, the howls behind them mingled with screams as the first to fall out were overrun. Tahrain raised his sweat-soaked head, and the nearness of the canyon surprised him. Already they were passing scrub grasses and mounds of dirt. In a few minutes they'd reach cover.

But there were no more minutes. The soldiers could run no farther. Nearly half the company had collapsed already. Tahrain called out to the half-orc, only a few steps in front of him. The barbarian pulled up short and looked back at his leader.

"Now—now's the time!"

Krusk shook his ugly head but Tahrain stopped his refusal with a curse.

"Now, damn it! You've got to get away. I'm going to die here regardless of what you do. My only hope lives with you."

He slammed his palm against Krusk's chest, where he knew the half-orc kept the packet.

But still Krusk refused to part. He gripped his greataxe and looked at Tahrain. When the two pairs of eyes met, Tahrain wondered how anyone could consider this misshapen creature anything but a valiant man.

"Go," Tahrain pleaded.

"Look out!"

The cry came suddenly and Tahrain whirled away from Krusk.

A mounted figure seemed almost to materialize out of the swirling dust and heat shimmers amid the remnants of his company. It drove in among the rearguard—a black horse, a rider clad all in black armor, and a sword upraised like Hextor's own. Tahrain had seen this figure from the city wall, commanding the assault.

Now the bastard's here, Tahrain thought, intent on killing what's left of my company.

Below the knight, a soldier from the rear guard struggled to draw her own weapon, but the knight's arm came down. The black sword fell just as the Kalpeshian's blade cleared its scabbard. The woman cried out as the black blade split her skull. Blood splattered the horse's side as the soldier collapsed into the sand.

The knight spurred the horse forward. Soldiers dived out of the destrier's path, or simply collapsed to the side. The knight ignored them. The full, black helmet fixed itself on Tahrain, as if the wearer suddenly knew who led the desperate company. The horse lunged.

Tahrain readied himself for the charge, but a hand grasped his shoulder and pulled him off-balance. He stumbled and fell. The knight swept over him, the horse's hooves missing his head by inches. He heard the beast stumble on the suddenly rocky ground. As the captain looked back, he saw the knight struggle to stay astride the animal as it tried not to fall or break a leg.

Rolling away and up, Tahrain turned toward his rescuer to tell him to obey orders and keep running, but then he saw the man's face. It wasn't Krusk, whom he'd expected, but Polrus. The half-orc was nowhere to be seen.

Polrus grinned feebly as the knight fought to turn the horse. "My turn, sir," he said. "Get going."

The lieutenant maneuvered so the knight would have to ride over him to keep Tahrain from escaping toward the canyon. He braced his shortspear for the charge.

The captain looked around. Krusk was gone. He'd obeyed orders, finally, and gotten away. Tahrain silently sent a quick prayer to Pelor to protect the half-orc then he drew his own weapon. It was a long-handled falchion and Tahrain gripped it in both hands. The howls of the gnolls grew closer.

"No, lieutenant. I'm staying with you. I've fulfilled my oath. Our mission goes on though we do not."

Nodding without fully understanding, Polrus turned toward the knight.

"Someday," he said wryly, "you'll have to tell me what all this is about."

Tahrain grinned.

The black knight stood over the bloody, arrow-filled corpses of Captain Tahrain and Lieutenant Polrus. Barks and howls sang out all around, and gnolls, some carrying bloodstained axes and others wielding crude bows, loped up to the armored figure.

"Any survivors?" asked the knight. The voice sounded almost musical, but also cold, even metallic.

The gnoll's tongue lolled in its mouth as it ducked its head. It bore two weapons, a hand axe and what looked like an oversized scimitar with a cruel, hooked end. A white patch of especially long fur adorned its canine head. Its ears had many notches—marks of challengers to the gnoll's dominance, all defeated.

It barked a reply in its own language.

"Good," the knight replied. "We'll question them, but we must hurry. I need to get back to the army before it disintegrates."

The gnoll howled quietly. It was almost a whimper.

"Don't worry; you'll have your fun. Make them talk. Find out if any escaped. If you can't get anything out of them. . . ." The knight toed Tahrain's corpse and the gnoll's answering bark took on a cruel, snickering tone. The blood from the captain's body had stopped flowing, but the sand all around it was mud-red. "Well, that's why I brought the shamans. You'll get answers. From them, or from him."

The gnoll bobbed its head and stepped back. The knight

crouched to look at the body. Gauntleted hands gracefully removed the black helmet. Long ebony hair spilled out and across armored shoulders and framed the narrow face of a severe, yet beautiful woman. Her blue eyes traveled up and down Tahrain's fallen form and her fingers felt along the blood-soaked raiment. For a moment, she gazed into the captain's dead, staring eyes, then she stood and walked away.

Krusk watched the slaughter from the relative safety of the canyon's rocky edge. He felt his rage grow until he could barely control it. He hugged the rock to stop himself from bursting forward when the captain dueled the black knight, and he pressed Tahrain's packet to his face when the man was struck down. Never had the half-orc done something so difficult, or that felt so shameful, as hiding while his only friend fought and died. Krusk knew that he couldn't have saved the captain, he couldn't even have saved himself if he'd been with the others. He would be dead, and the woman in the black armor would have Tahrain's papers and the golden disk. If not for his promise, that's how Krusk would have wanted it.

From the rocks, Krusk marked the dark warrior and the gnolls, memorizing their faces and voices. He would take the packet to the place Tahrain described, with or without help, and he would keep his promise. Then, with his oath fulfilled, Krusk would see the knight and the gnolls again.

He would see them again.

THE HUNT

The rain slackened as the hunters made their way through the forest, but the light continued to dim. Early tripped over two logs and what Naull thought may have been a hedgehog, but neither Ian nor Regdar would agree to light torches.

"Ian can see the tracks just fine," Regdar said shortly when the wizard brought the subject up for the third time, "and I can see him. The rest of you follow me and we'll make it."

Naull silently cursed her partner's stubbornness, but privately agreed it was the wise choice. Orcs, she knew, could see well in the dark—but only over short distances. If the party lit a torch, anybody within a hundred yards would see them coming.

"He's slowing down," Ian said suddenly, stopping short. Regdar nearly stumbled over the half-elf and Naull bumped into him, her small body banging against the hard metal of his armor. Trebba put a hand out and Early—now well in the back of the party—managed to hold up. "He's stopped fleeing. He's going more carefully."

Is that a good thing, or a bad thing? Naull thought.

She brushed her black, wet hair back from her eyes and looked around. Trees, nothing but trees. She didn't like the seeming openness. A human through-and-through, she still preferred "adventuring" in caves. The woods looked open and boundless, but all those trees could be hiding eyes, and bows, and arrows.

"Spread out a little," Regdar ordered.

Everyone, except Ian, who still searched for the fugitive orc leader's tracks, obeyed automatically. Naull couldn't help but smile a little. She'd known Regdar for quite some time, but the others had been with them for only four days. She hardly knew anything about them, and they knew a little about her and her partner, yet they followed his direction almost without question. She'd trusted Regdar for a long time, but why did they? Naull looked over each of her companions in turn as they searched the darkness for signs of their foe.

Trebba, a self-professed thief, picked her way up the slick angle of a fallen tree, probably in hopes of getting a look around in the dim light. She moved gracefully, even over the damp, moss-covered bark. Soon she was nothing but a shadow against the broken trunk.

Off to the other side, a branch snapped and a soft, pained curse followed—Early. The tall man had joined up with them at the village, and Naull knew for certain that he was a local. He couldn't have been more than eighteen years old. He had no beard and chubby cheeks, but he was very, very strong. The "boy" had submitted to a few tests before being accepted as part of the group. Lightly armored and wielding nothing but a wooden shield and an old, plain long sword, he'd nearly broken through Regdar's well-trained guard with nothing but strength and enthusiasm. Naull watched him pick his way around a broken tree limb, trying not to make any more noise. He started looking around, squinting into the darkness, as if foes might leap out from behind any tree.

Green, Naull thought, but Early's actions reminded her she had work to do, too. She did a quick inventory of her spell pouches and sighed. She still had everything she needed to cast her remaining spells, but her "big bangs" were gone, used up in the ambush that afternoon. Her web spell had snared most of the orcs at one swoop—all but their leader, who sacrificed his troops to make his own escape. They were tracking that lone orc through the darkening woods, hoping it would lead them to its lair, what remained of the raiding party, and their spoils.

Scanning the woods, Naull tried to locate Ian and Regdar. She found them both quickly. Regdar, the burly fighter who led the group, was easy to spot in his plate armor. He stood almost motionless over Ian.

The half-elf, on the other hand, was an enigma. Except for his chosen vocation—his woodcraft spoke to his part-elven background—he didn't act like any half-elf she'd heard about or met before. An abrasive mercenary by his own admission, the slight, short man still had a compelling, almost intense, nature. Even his name was strange. Elves, in Naull's limited experience, usually had longer, more sing-song names. "Ian" seemed too plain, somehow.

Ian's light hair and white skin, however, went along with Naull's image of elves. The fact that his clothes somehow stayed inexplicably clean as he searched the dark ground for tracks fit, too. His sharp, ice-blue eyes pierced the darkness and turned toward Naull. He'd sensed her staring at him, she knew suddenly, and he held her gaze for a moment, then turned back to his work.

It never crossed her mind that Ian wouldn't find the tracks, even in the dark, even after the brief rain shower, and that proved a good instinct. After only a few minutes, the ranger stood up again and motioned the party in.

"He's gotten away," Ian said flatly. Early cursed, but Regdar waited and watched the half-elf pause. "Or so he thinks."

A rare smile graced the ranger's features, but it wasn't a pleasant one. The smile was that of a hunter who enjoyed the kill and who knew his quarry had been run to ground.

"I wanted to make sure he hadn't gotten clever, but I'm convinced he thinks we're still back at the ambush site, picking through

the wagons and his fellows' gear. It's what he'd be doing, probably."
Nothing disguised the disdain in Ian's voice. But the half-elf grew
professional again, turned toward a nearby slope, and said, "He
paused here and looked around. He didn't hear us coming." A sharp
look made Early blush, but Ian continued, "and he couldn't see us.
We were just far enough behind to make him feel confident, so he
headed down there."

"Back toward the path?" Trebba asked.

"Yes," he replied. "The path probably leads right up near their
lair. Nobody comes this deep into these woods anymore," he
added. "They didn't have to hide."

Regdar nodded and asked, "Should we go back to the path, or
do you want to follow him directly?"

"The orcs obviously didn't think they'd be followed far into the
forest. We found the path after only, what, two days of looking?"
Ian continued, not waiting for confirmation. "They stayed careful until they got into the woods, but then they relaxed. I'm guessing they got sloppier the nearer they got to home."

"So we should go back to the path," Early drawled confidently,
"find 'em quick, and kick some orc tail. Heat up the oven 'cause
we'll be back for breakfast."

He patted his long sword and grinned.

"Well," the half-elf drawled, mocking the farm boy's accent
until Regdar's sharp glance cowed the ranger. "If we go back onto
the path, we'll almost certainly find the orcs' lair—and probably
quicker than if we follow the tracks of a single orc through the
forest at night, in this drizzle, but then we'd be coming at them
from where they expect. As I've already said, this one we're tracking thinks he fooled us. If we go back, we're doing what he
expects—and night is orc time."

"So what?" Early asked, a tiny bit of belligerence creeping into
his voice. "There's just the one o' him left. We already killed over
a half-dozen orcs in the ambush. If you're thinkin' about Yurgen,
well, I'm sorry he's dead, too, but he did a foolish thing, charging

into the woods alone after this brute. If he'd done like Regdar told him, he'd still be alive. I don't care how tough this orc is, I'm bettin' the five of us can take one more."

As Ian opened his mouth for a scathing reply, he found it hard to talk with two hundred and fifty plus pounds of plate-armored human standing on his toe. The half-elf gasped and Regdar stepped back.

"But consider this, Early," Regdar said as if nothing had happened, "there may be more than just the one we're tracking."

"There certainly will be," Ian grumbled, flexing his mashed toes. "They've been operating out of that lair for a month now. This isn't just a hit-and-run raiding party. I'd guess that at least a couple of warriors stayed behind to guard the other loot, plus whatever others tagged along—young and such. They could still be strong enough to cause us some trouble if they catch us by surprise, or if we just stumble into their midst in the dark." Ian waved back toward the ambush site, several miles behind them and grinned. "Remember how well it worked for us."

Early nodded in understanding and grinned back. Naull looked between the two of them, thinking perhaps the half-elf wasn't as cold as he seemed, and the farm boy wasn't as dumb as he acted.

We all put on our little shows, she thought.

"Hey, Naull," Regdar asked. "What about you? What's our wizard got?"

"Well . . ." she started, fingers automatically going to her component pouches, even though she'd just sorted them out moments before, "not a lot. Don't worry about light. I can take care of that in a hurry, when we need it. And I might be able to distract one or two with some sounds."

"What about the big stuff?" Early asked impatiently.

She realized suddenly that her web spell may have been the most magic he'd ever seen. A lot of country folk had clerics to tend to their ills, but wizards preferred the city life. Books didn't grow on trees, after all.

She chuckled at her inadvertent joke. Early took it to mean she had something nasty prepared and he nodded.

"Got it. You don't wanna spoil the surprise. No problem."

He gave her a thumbs up and started off. Ian and Trebba already followed the orc's tracks, but Regdar hung back.

"Seriously, Naull," he asked in a low voice, "what do you have left?"

She sighed, "Well, I've got another magic missile, but everything else is pretty defensive. Not everybody can walk around in their own private golem, you know." She slugged his armored side in an attempt at playfulness and was rewarded with a dull clang. "*Ow!*" As she pretended to suck her knuckles in pain, Regdar grinned.

"Can't blame you for that. I wish we had a healer with us," Regdar sighed. He pulled off one of his gauntlets and put his hand on her back, gently guiding her over and around the underbrush as they walked. "It wouldn't have done Yurgen any good, but . . ."

He went quiet as the two of them followed the rest of the party.

"You couldn't have stopped him, Regdar," she said. She reached around and gave his bare hand a squeeze. "He shouldn't have done what he did, but he died fighting."

"That's the best we can hope for, I suppose," Regdar said.

"Not me! I'm going to die in a big bed at the top of my own wizard's tower, surrounded by dozens of spellbooks and served by hundreds of apprentices!" She smiled lazily and winked. "Maybe you can be captain of my guard, if you play your cards right."

She ran the fingers of her free hand over her tunic, fingering a few of her component pouches. Naull knew the cut of the pouch belts helped accentuate her modest curves and she was surprised to find herself flirting.

He's my partner! she thought, a little embarrassed, but she smiled at the fighter anyway.

Looking down at her, Regdar answered her smile with one of his own. His close-cropped goatee sometimes gave him a violent, even evil look, but now it nearly made Naull laugh out loud.

"If I have time for it," he said. "I figure I'll be a king and you'll be my court wizard . . . or jester. Depends on if you ever get better at this spell business."

He let go of her hand and raised his arm in mock defense as Naull swiped at him again.

"I guess I'm getting used to this ironmongery after all," he teased as he nimbly avoided another blow. He caught her wrist, lightly, on the third. "C'mon," he said, his voice serious again. "It isn't over yet."

Naull straightened at the change in his voice and she nodded.

Back to business, she thought.

"You're right. Best not wear the crown till they make you king."

It took the party less than another hour to track the orc leader the rest of the way to his lair. Ian was right—the orcs settled in after their first few raids and looked comfortable. They laired in a small valley in the woods, a dell with good tree cover and caves in the northern side. If there were guards, they weren't there now. Perhaps the leader called them in when he arrived ahead of them. Night lay full upon them, and the party moved in a tight, quiet mass.

"Whew!" exclaimed Early. "The smell!"

"Shut up!" Regdar hissed. Early's voice sounded loud in the still darkness. "Everyone, hold up."

Ian crouched near a tree, running his pale fingers up and down the trunk. In the gloom, Naull saw his bright eyes follow his hands, then his whole face turned upward. He pointed and her eyes followed his finger.

Trebba, moving gracefully and silently over the leaf and twig covered ground, came up to Ian's tree and began climbing. The woman moved slowly at first, but seemingly found the going easier than she'd expected. Within a few seconds her black shape disappeared over the object in the tree. A few seconds after that a knotted rope slid down the trunk and into their midst.

Early grabbed the end of the rope and steadied it for Ian. The elf climbed it nimbly and soon he was gone. Naull wondered if she should follow, but at a sign from Regdar, Early and the rope slid up against the tree trunk, putting it between them and the dell.

Ian and Trebba returned after a minute or two, and the party huddled behind the tree.

Regdar turned to Ian and asked, "Could you see the lair?"

"Yes. They've cleared away a lot of the trees and brush down there. We missed a path they use to bring in their loot; it's in the southeast corner. Their leader knows the area well enough he didn't have to head for it," the half-elf explained. "They've got a rough barricade on it, but I guess they anticipated success. Most of it's been cleared away. Near as I can tell from here, they have a couple wagons filled with junk lying on the road now. Two or three strong orcs could move them, but not quickly. It looks pretty muddy down there."

"Trebba?"

The woman shrugged and said, "Ian saw more than I did. It's dark down there. We're all going to need light if we're going in. I don't know as much about orcs as our ranger here—" Ian snorted at the compliment as if it meant nothing, but he didn't interrupt— "but it'd be simple to place a few traps or alarms on the likely approaches. Even sharp sticks covered with leaves'd give 'em some advantage."

Ian added, "Orcs like nasty little foot- and spring-traps, coated with their own feces or whatever poisons they can find. They'll be unpleasant." He waved his hand in a broad arc. "I'd expect they've got surprises littering the slopes all the way in."

"Why? I thought you said they ain't watching out," Early asked. He pointed to the platform above their heads. "No guards. Most of 'em went out on the raid, right? They ain't worried about anybody finding their camp, you said."

The half-elf answered with surprising patience, "Just because they don't expect anyone to find their nest doesn't mean they haven't prepared."

"Right," Trebba filled in. "Step on a caltrop or spring a rope trap and you're going to make noise. Whatever we do, Regdar—" she turned to the fighter—"we'd better be careful."

"And we'd best get going," Ian urged. "That leader's pretty steamed, or he will be. He's had a little more than an hour to think about what happened to him and his warriors, and he's going to realize he got away because there just weren't enough of us to take him. He's either going to want revenge or he'll want to get out of here quick."

"How'll he plan revenge? I doubt he'd know where to find us." Naull asked.

"He doesn't have to find us," Regdar answered. "Orcs don't like even fights."

"He'll try to take revenge against the village," Trebba added, dread in her voice.

Early's eyes widened and the big man cursed.

"He's not in any shape to do anything tonight," Naull cautioned. "We could wait until morning."

Regdar shifted uncomfortably as Trebba and Early nodded. Ian didn't look happy, either.

"What?" Naull asked. "Am I missing something?"

The ranger and the fighter exchanged glances.

"He won't try to get revenge tonight, no matter what," Regdar said slowly, "but he might try to get away."

Naull started to say that was fine with her, but both Trebba and Early jumped in.

"Get away? No!" the dark woman said.

"With all that treasure!" Early cried.

Both had their points, Naull conceded. Trebba wanted revenge for Yurgen, and Early,—along with Regdar and Ian, it seemed— wanted what they all thought was the better part of their payment. Their contract with the village was fifty gold apiece, plus any of the humanoids' loot they could recover. Even modest estimates put the potential treasure at well over a thousand gold pieces, based on what they'd heard about the earlier raids. The wizard got a sinking feeling in her stomach.

"Surely," she said, "we could at least wait until morning?"

Shrugging, Regdar looked down at Ian. The half-elf delivered the bad news.

"These orcs have been here a while. It would be just like them to have dug out a few more exits from their lair. It's a long time till dawn. If the orc leader thinks we're on his trail, or just doesn't want to hang around now that we've wiped out one of his war bands, they could slip out a tunnel we know nothing about."

No one in the party looked particularly happy with the thought of following the orc leader into his den in the middle of the night, but Naull was particularly unhappy about it.

"I really don't have much more in the spell department," she said again.

"Chances are good," Regdar answered, "that there aren't many orcs left in there. Like Ian said, an orc leader's going to want to keep his warriors close. He probably took nearly all of them out on the raid."

The fighter didn't sound like he'd convinced himself of that, but Naull looked at the faces of the rest of the party. They'd lost a comrade and didn't seem in the mood for rational thought.

"All right, then. What's the plan?"

Ian could see the best in darkness, so he was to head down the slope first. They chose to approach the lair from the southwest, mainly because it looked like the easiest way down, except for the path past the wagons. No one wanted to go that way. If there were any guards, they'd be there. To the north were the caves themselves, and the slope became a cliff that way. They had no doubt that with ropes and Trebba's assistance they could climb down and perhaps surprise the orcs from above, but since orcs could see in the dark and they couldn't, they'd be more likely to be spotted and shot full of arrows before they could retreat.

Trebba would go with Ian. She told the rest of the party to stay back as far as they could and follow their footsteps exactly, but she felt—and everyone else agreed—that she'd have the best chance of spotting a trap before stepping in it than anyone. It would be slow going, but the trees and underbrush provided plenty of cover.

Naull worried about that. What if they were wrong about guards? Orcs could be behind every tree between here and the caves—more than a hundred yards away, if Ian was right—and it would be a simple matter for outlying pickets to let them enter and shut the trap behind them. When she brought this up, though, Regdar's answer was less than satisfying.

"Ian thinks it's unlikely, and we'll have to risk it. I think he's right that the orcs wouldn't leave many warriors behind to guard their loot, just because of the trust issue. If that's true, there can't be more than a handful of warriors down there."

Define "handful," Naull mused glumly.

She was to try to stay in the middle of the party, right in front of Early, with Regdar bringing up the rear. They'd used the last of their coalblack on his plate armor and the two fighters' swords in an effort to minimize any reflection there might be in the dim light, but nothing could cover the clanking Regdar made when he moved at any speed. They hoped the orcs wouldn't notice until the vanguard was upon them.

If I'd known we were going to be sneaking around, the wizard thought sourly, I would've brought along a silence spell.

She made a mental note to ask more questions before she prepared her spells every morning. "Are we likely to be storming an orc lair in the pitch darkness tonight?" hadn't seemed like a pertinent question eighteen hours before.

Despite her sour thoughts, Naull kept her concentration following in Early's footsteps. She let a part of her mind review her spells again, desperate to come up with a combination that might deal with any surprises. Still, she just didn't have anything that would be much help against more orcs than they hoped to face.

Suddenly, Ian froze. In the gloom, Naull saw him grasp Trebba's shoulder and the thief held out both her hands and crouched down. It was the signal they'd agreed upon to indicate "Stop!"

Whether the cloud cover broke a little, letting the moon's light in just a tiny bit more, or whether cold Wee Jas chose to look down with uncharacteristic kindness on one of her less-devoted servants, Naull found she could make out the half-elf and what lay just beyond him. A damp wind blew through the dell. The light continued to grow as the cloud cover moved away. With a start of surprise Naull realized that she could see the cave mouth they were heading toward. It lay to the left, recessed into the northernmost wall of the valley. Naull could almost feel orc archers waiting there in the complete darkness of the cave mouth, but no arrows flew.

After a minute or more of silent waiting and watching, Ian motioned the others forward again. As Naull closed in, she heard Trebba's whisper.

"I want to check it out," the thief said. "There could still be a trap in the entrance, or an alarm of some kind."

Ian shrugged and prepared to go with her.

"Don't ring any doorbells," he joked.

"Go ahead," Naull whispered. "I'll get Early and Regdar to move up. We can get to the cave mouth quickly from here if you need us."

Trebba nodded and moved off into the shadows.

"Be careful," Naull added.

She wondered if it was too late for any of them to be careful enough, but she drove the thought as far out of her mind as possible.

THE LAIR

Trebba and Ian disappeared into the cave mouth, and for a few short, agonizing moments, Naull, Early, and Regdar crouched in the darkness.

Ian soon appeared in the dim light outside the cave mouth. He stood nearly erect and waved. By their pre-arranged plan, Early started forward, moving quickly up to the cliff wall then along the edge to where the ranger stood. Naull waited until Early passed the orcs' septic hole and followed. Regdar came last.

Naull gave a sharp intake of breath as she arrived at the cave mouth. Trebba sat with her back against the rough stone wall, her hand clutched to her right shoulder. The thief was in obvious pain. Her breasts rose and fell with labored breathing.

"I'm all right. I'm all right," she chanted.

Beside her lay a bloody bolt and what looked like a few yards of string.

When Regdar arrived, Ian said, "Trebba found a tripwire strung across the entrance. It would've sounded some sort of alarm. She disabled it, but then that—" the half-elf pointed to the dart on the ground—"shot out of the ceiling. It would've gotten her right in the top of the skull, but she twisted out of the way."

"Not far enough," Trebba gasped. "But I'm all right. Help me up."

The rogue stood with Regdar's assistance. Early looked at the wound while Ian studied the arrow.

"Nasty," the big man said, "but it's clean. Good job." He inclined his head to Ian.

"I don't think the bolt was poisoned," Ian replied. "Or if it was, the poison lost its effect, sitting up there for so long."

"Thanks ever so much, guys," Trebba said with disdain.

She moved her pack's straps over to her uninjured shoulder.

"You all right?" Regdar asked. "You could wait here."

Trebba shook her head and answered, "No. If there's more traps in there, you're going to need someone to find them."

Early looked into the darkness and said, "I can't see more than my hand in front of my face."

In answer, Naull drew a few items out of her pouches.

"Better than torches," Regdar agreed.

A few murmured words later and an eye-sized stone in the wizard's hand lit up with a heatless flame like that of a torch. One smooth motion later, Naull had the stone affixed to a small, cheap ring. She opened and closed her hand over it a few times, illuminating the cave mouth and dimming it to near-darkness again in the process.

"Nice trick," Early said. "I seen light spells, o'course, but that ring's handy."

"Keeps my hands free but lets me cut off the light if we need to." Naull took the ring off and handed it to Trebba. "If you're going first, though, you'll need it."

The rogue nodded and took the ring. The party headed in; Trebba first, shielding the light as much as she could. Regdar and Ian followed, and lastly Naull and Early came side-by-side.

In truth, Naull expected the cave to simply open into one large cavern, but she realized quickly that that wasn't going to happen. The orcs were lucky in their choice of lairs. The cave turned into a tunnel that twisted and fell away to the right almost immediately. Trebba uncovered and disabled another alarm or trap—she didn't bother telling them which it was—and the party started moving a little more quickly.

The passage wound away and down for perhaps a hundred more feet. In the dim light, they could see the next turn, the next dive, and then nothing. The ranger reached out and grasped the rogue's belt, stopping her short.

"Shh . . . listen."

As one, the party held its breath. They heard noises that sounded like speech, coming from ahead of them.

Trebba moved forward alone, returning a few moments later.

"There's an intersection up there, and some light coming from around the right corner. To the left it's dark, but it goes up really steeply. I didn't see or hear anything, but I couldn't look around without moving into the open."

Regdar nodded.

"Trebba, Ian, you take point," he said. "I bet the orcs're around that way to the right and that's their living area, but there may be some up and to the left. Be careful." He turned to Early and Naull and continued, "Early, you go next, with me right behind. When we see around the corner, if it is the main orc lair, I'm gonna want you—" Regdar pointed to the big man there—"to get up front with me in a hurry. Trebba, you drop back with Naull and make sure nothing comes down on us from the left. If things look clear, you can start shooting into the main cavern, but keep those arrows out of our backs."

Naull smiled slightly at the fighter's joke but she knew he was in earnest.

Trebba started to move away, but Regdar grabbed her hand and said, "If Ian is right, we'll have a more or less even fight on our hands. I want to get into the cavern, if that's what it is, as quickly as possible. Most of us're more maneuverable than the orcs, but I don't want any surprises. Something drops down from that other passage, shout your head off. They'll know we're here if that happens anyway."

"All right."

As Trebba and Ian moved forward, Early watched but Regdar hesitated.

"What do you think, Naull?" he asked in a voice too quiet for anyone but the small woman to hear.

"It's a decent plan," she answered nervously. "I hope Ian is right about the orcs, though, or we could be headed for trouble."

Regdar shook his head. He doesn't want to do this, either, she thought suddenly. She almost asked him again to call the whole attack off, but the moment passed.

As the party approached, the sounds grew in volume. Foul orc speech and cursing came from the passage to the right, and they saw the firelight flicker on the uneven stone. Trebba skillfully slipped up around the corner and back again. In the dim light she nodded and held up five fingers.

Regdar and Early moved up. Early had his long sword and shield ready, but Regdar bent and strung his large bow.

With a glance up the passage to the left, the two fighters went around the corner. A shout of surprise from the orcs greeted them, and Regdar's bow twanged. The arrow took a heavyset orc in the chest. He spun around in place and fell, right near the fire.

"That's four to go!" Early shouted.

He started rushing forward and Regdar, dropping his bow, swept out his sword, and followed.

The melee that ensued was fast and brutal. Early and Regdar barreled into the remaining orcs at full speed. Though the brutes had their gear on and their weapons out, they weren't prepared for two large humans—one nearly seven feet tall and screaming like a madman and the other encased almost entirely in blackened plate armor and wielding a sword almost as long as he was tall—attacking them in their lair. They gave ground quickly. When Ian entered the fray, one orc threw down its weapon and turned to run.

With a yelp, the orc sprawled on its face, one of Ian's small axes buried in its back. In a flash Ian yanked a second axe from his belt and rushed forward to duel with a big orc. Its two-handed axe blows cleft nothing but air as the half-elf played with his prey. When the orc tossed a quick glance over its shoulder toward the exit, the tip of the half-elf's rapier thrust forward and pierced the orc through the neck.

Naull watched both the battle and the dark passage leading up. She thought about casting her last light spell up there, but Trebba had the ring out and she could see the hole in the "ceiling" that led to an upper area. Nothing stirred up there, so Naull turned back to the fight.

With three orcs down in only twice as many seconds, the fight was nearly over. Early and Regdar each fought to keep the last few humanoids at bay, but they didn't want them to escape, either. Beyond the fire they could see another passage—a large, dark cave mouth. If the two fled down there, who knew how long it would take to catch them. Better to finish the last of them off in the open, rather than hunt them through their warren.

The last of them? Naull thought.

She scanned the three—now four, as Early's foe was down, too—orc corpses in the room. She glanced up at the last just as Regdar drove his bastard sword into its guts.

No, that's not the leader, either, she concluded.

She'd seen the leader only briefly back at the ambush site, but none of these orcs were nearly as well armed and armored as he had been. She wouldn't forget that two-handed cleaver anytime soon.

"Regdar!" she called out to tell him, but then Trebba screamed.

By bad coincidence, both women were paying attention to the battle and not the hole at just the wrong time. As if they'd known of the watchers' distraction, two large orcs sprang down through the chute. One right after the other bore down on the wizard and the rogue. The first drove the point of a longspear into Trebba's stomach as she turned back to face them. The dark woman collapsed sideways with a gasp, blocking the passage for a precious second. Naull leaped back before she could suffer a similar fate.

The wizard found herself alone at the top of the passage facing two huge orcs. Up close, their yellow fangs looked huge and their breath stank of rotten meat. One croaked evilly as it twisted its spear in Trebba's stomach and she whimpered on the ground, rolling away. The other swept a cruelly familiar two-handed sword from its back sheath and stepped toward Naull.

The wizard fell backward, holding one hand up as if in futile defense, but the sound that escaped the small woman's lips wasn't a scream. The sword came down hard, but sheared off at the last second as it struck a magical, invisible shield. Naull tried to back-step and she tumbled backward into the larger room.

The orc with the spear wrenched it out of Trebba's body, then leaped past Naull and down toward the fighters. Regdar turned when Trebba screamed and cried out with rage, starting back up the passage. The orc stabbed at the more lightly-armored Early. Trebba's blood spattered the man's wooden shield as it turned the blow aside, but Early's riposte also flew wide. The orc spun in place and brought the back of the spear around like a club, striking the big man in the sword arm and causing him to cry out in pain and drop his weapon.

Just then, a roar erupted from the cave beyond the fire. Ian had said no orc leader would leave many of his followers in a cave alone with their captured loot, and he hadn't been wrong. Five orc warriors had stayed behind along with the spear-wielder and now the party saw why. The orc "leader" was merely a lieutenant.

The creature erupting from the cave mouth had to be the humanoids' true commander.

It had the jutting chin and fangs of an orc, but stood nearly half again as tall. Its bare, elongated arms hung down past its tree trunk thighs and below its perpetually bent knees. Gold and silver along with bone and hide ornamented its brown, stringy hair, and it wielded a huge club covered in spikes and wrapped with leather thongs.

"An ogre!" Ian cried out in dismay.

The ogre bellowed and started toward the ranger. Ian was farthest into the cavern, almost up to the fire after his duel with the orc, and it was obvious the creature wanted the closest target first.

Naull struggled to rise to her feat, to do anything to help, but she had to roll away as the sword-wielding orc lieutenant bounded toward her. Thankfully the orc didn't reach her. Regdar jumped between them and the two huge weapons rang against each other. The orc had the momentum, and Regdar's sword bounced back.

"Naull, if you've got any surprises hidden, now would be a good time!"

The wizard chose quickly. Not even bothering to stand up, she rose to her knees and pointed at the orc fighting Regdar. Two bright missiles, like those that had killed an orc at the ambush, streaked from her fingertips and struck the brutish lieutenant full in the chest. He lurched backward and roared, but didn't fall.

Regdar screamed in frustration and struck with his bastard sword. The orc tried to parry but the blow pushed the creature's own blade back across its chest and the edge of Regdar's weapon bit into the humanoid's bicep. Blood from a deep cut flowed down its arm.

The orc backstepped but ran up against the cavern's wall. It didn't try going up and to the left. Even without Trebba's body in the way, stepping up on the uneven ground might have brought catastrophe. It had no choice but to answer Regdar, blow for blow. The two dueled as Naull watched, feeling helpless. She looked around for anything that might save them.

Across the entrance, Early battled bravely against the spear-wielding orc, but he was obviously overmatched. He'd drawn his backup weapon, a dagger, but no matter how he tried he couldn't get close enough to use it. Every time he pushed inside the orc's reach, the spear turned and the orc walloped him with the wooden butt. It didn't cause him much pain, but it backed him up. Meanwhile, the pointed end of the weapon had jabbed Early twice, once in the thigh and once in the shoulder. The big man was tiring and there was nothing Naull could do.

All this seemed like a sideline, though, when the wizard looked down into the cavern. The ogre bellowed its fierce war cry and drove at Ian. With a cry of his own, the ranger leaped forward and somehow managed to get inside his foe's reach. Stabbing upward with his rapier, he pierced its thick hide. Before the ogre could bring a two-handed smash down on the ranger's head, the half-elf leaped away again.

What can I do? Naull thought wildly.

She saw her friends fighting losing battles and she tried to clear her head. It still rang from hitting the cave floor and she despaired. Even if she thought of some way to help, what did she have that might make a difference? If only she could get one of them free from an opponent long enough to help another—two on one could make the difference. She just needed to think.

"Everything else is pretty much defensive," she'd said to Regdar before they came on this cursed hunt. "Not everybody can walk around in their own private golem," she'd joked. Grimly, she recalled her words. Then her eyes widened and she looked around.

Regdar ... Regdar has the best chance of helping anyone, she thought. Boccob, may my magic be blessed! And, she added, Wee Jas, if I die doing this, bring me back to avenge my friends' deaths!

Naull cast two spells in quick succession. With one, her form grew blurry and indistinct. The other yielded no visible signs of effect, but she knew it had worked just the same.

Drawing her own tiny dagger, Naull leaped to Regdar's side and shouted, "Help the others! I can handle this one!"

Regdar spared her a glance of amazement and looked ready to argue. She physically shoved him—she knew she didn't have enough strength to move the man, but she tried all the same.

"Move! Before it's too late. I know what I'm doing!"

Taking her at her word, the fighter backed away. The orc lieutenant grimaced and said something in a guttural tongue she was glad she couldn't understand.

"Come on, then," Naull answered grimly, brandishing her dagger as if it was a weapon of power. "I haven't got all night. If I don't kill you before dawn, I'll never get my eight hours in."

Whether the orc understood her or not, it seemed outraged by her defiant gesture. Gripping its sword in both hands, it struck at the small wizard with a blow that surely would have cloven her from crown to crotch, if it had landed. But the blade sheared off as it approached Naull's blurred form and clanged against the stone at her feet. The combination of protective spells would be enough to hold the orc off, at least for a short time. Naull hoped it would be long enough.

Regdar, in the meantime, bounded into the cavern, taking a wild swing at Early's orc as he passed. The creature ducked the blow easily, but the sudden assault distracted the creature long enough for the farm boy-turned-adventurer to slam his shield against the creature's flat face. The orc staggered back and tripped, stumbling against the wall. Early slashed with all his considerable strength at the creature, severing its spear haft and burying his weapon deep in the orc's chest. Orc and man tumbled to the floor a moment later, one exhausted, the other dead.

"Early! Get out of here!" Regdar shouted as he moved toward the ogre. "Get Trebba! Help Naull! We can't fight this!"

Whether or not Regdar believed they could fight the ogre, Ian hadn't given up yet. Snarling, the ranger dived in and out of the ogre's reach, jabbing it with his rapier. The giant howled and bled from many tiny pinpricks, but its massive club came closer to Ian's head with every swipe.

"Over here!" Regdar called.

He stood close to the fire pit, his bastard sword gripped tightly in both hands.

Naull, who could see the fight with the ogre even as she parried and dodged the orc lieutenant's blows, wondered whether her partner had called out to Ian or the ogre. Regardless of his intent, the ogre turned and lurched toward him. Perhaps it saw a potentially easier target. Wrapped in heavy armor, the fighter couldn't possibly move as fast as the annoying half-elf.

For a moment, that put the ogre between the ranger and the fighter. As Regdar stepped back quickly to avoid the swinging club, Ian also jumped back, hurling his hand axe at the ogre's back.

The creature howled in pain and anger as the hand axe bit deep into its well-muscled back. Just as it started to turn, however, Regdar thrust his broad-bladed sword into the fire pit's ashes and flung them up into the ogre's face. Sparks and cinders blinded the creature and it dropped its club to paw at its eyes.

Naull almost cried in relief as she saw Ian scamper around the maddened ogre and that nearly proved her undoing. The orc swung its blade in a wide arc, striking the wizard a glancing blow on her side. If not for her shield and mage armor spells, the cleaver would have cut her in two. As it was, she felt herself smashed against the cave wall, pinned and helpless. The orc grinned evilly and leaned down to finish her off.

Then Trebba sat up.

Early had struggled to the thief's side and bound her wounds, but when the ogre screamed the man had started back down into the cavern, leaving her on her own. Trebba stood shakily and lurched forward. Naull, even as she felt fear and horror at the thought of dying at the orc lieutenant's hands, looked over the creature's shoulder and felt pity as she saw blood leaking down from the thief's lips. Then she saw the dagger in the woman's upraised hand.

The orc drew back for a final blow but grunted in surprise. Trebba's dagger caught it squarely between the shoulder blades. The creature dropped its cleaver, put both hands behind its back, and fell forward, brushing against Naull as it died.

Stumbling against the sudden weight, Naull twisted away and looked up to see Trebba collapse onto her knees. Blood flowed freely from her mouth, and in the light of the spell her dark skin had a grayish cast.

"Pick her up!" Naull commanded.

Early stooped without a word and hefted Trebba into his arms.

Naull looked back, and to her dismay saw that neither Regdar nor Ian had moved entirely away from the ogre. They were both on her side of the creature, and it was obviously still blind and roaring in pain. Somehow it had struck Regdar in the side and Naull could see the dent in his armor from twenty feet away. Ian was shouting and waving his arms—one hand a bloody mess— trying to distract the ogre as the fighter stumbled away.

Naull ran to Regdar and put his heavy arm across her shoulders. He didn't put much weight on her, which the wizard took as a good sign.

He's just got the wind knocked out of him, she thought as they stumbled up and out of the cavern.

Crack! The ogre had retrieved its club and the wood smashed against stone. Ian tossed one more taunt then tumbled away from the big monster. He sprinted across the cavern and toward the entrance.

"Let's get out of here!" he said as he put Regdar's other arm across his shoulders.

The half-elf bled from a shallow wound on his scalp but

looked as if he could still run. They stepped over the body of the spear-wielding orc and ran as best they could toward the entrance. The ogre's cries of pain and rage followed them but didn't seem to grow any closer.

"Will it follow?" Naull asked as they neared the entrance to the caves.

The sky had cleared slightly and Naull could see the faint outline of the cave mouth ahead. She'd seen smears of blood—Early's or Trebba's—as they came, but there was no sign of either of them.

Regdar had a hard enough time running in his damaged armor and didn't answer.

Ian shrugged and said, "I don't know. Probably. I can't have blinded it permanently."

He looked down at the ranger, shrugged off everyone's assistance, and said, "I can walk. We must get moving. If we can make it to the road . . ."

The half-elf winced as they stumbled into the open air. As the three helped each other along, Naull felt two of her three protective spells fade. She looked back at the cave mouth but it was too dark inside to see anything. If the ogre caught them in the open, her mage armor wouldn't keep her from ending up as so much paste on the creature's bludgeon.

They passed the broken wagons the orcs had used for a barricade and Ian paused.

"Early and Trebba," he said. "They came this way, too." The ranger pointed at a small patch of blood and picked up a torn piece of cloth, probably from Early's tunic. "They shouldn't be too far ahead of us."

"At least Trebba's still alive," Naull said hopefully. "Did you see her stab that orc?"

Neither man answered. Naull looked back over her shoulder again. Nothing. She started to breathe a little easier.

The wizard breathed a lot easier a few minutes later. They'd picked their way around more debris—pieces from the broken wagons, empty casks, and discarded, rotting food—and finally reached the main road. This far into the woods, the "road" wasn't more than a well-beaten path, wide enough for two men to walk abreast. A few yards away, they saw Early crouching by Trebba. Naull looked at Regdar and Ian, and ran forward.

"Early! Is she . . . ?"

The big man looked up, tears in his eyes, then back down at the woman he'd carried up from the caves. Trebba had a crude bandage wrapped around her midsection, bloodstained white against her dark skin. Naull looked at Trebba's face. Early had cleaned it somehow, but only after. The thief was dead.

"H-her wounds," Early stammered. "I couldn't do nothin'. She tol' me t'leave her, but I thought she was just being . . ."

"Heroic?"

It was Ian. He'd walked up behind Naull. His wide, elf eyes shimmered in the darkness, and his pale face reflected the starlight.

"She was," he said, placing a hand on Early's shoulder.

"We've got to keep moving," Regdar said. His face was grim, but Naull could see the grief behind the mask. "Ian, take point. Naull, Early, go side-by-side. I'll bring up the rear."

Ian nodded and started forward. He'd spent a few moments wrapping his burned hand in another bandage, but he moved with obvious pain. Early bent to pick up Trebba's body.

"No, Early," Regdar said flatly. "Leave her."

Early turned and started to snarl, but Regdar didn't let him speak.

"She died to help get us out of there. If that ogre comes on us now, we're finished. You want her sacrifice to mean anything? Leave her."

The big man bristled, then he seemed to collapse in on himself and he nodded. Sword in hand, he turned away and followed Ian.

Naull started to say something to Regdar, but he met her eyes and frowned. His pain was obvious, but it only matched hers. *This isn't the way to earn a wizard's tower, is it?* she thought with more than a little irony.

She caught up to Early and they walked in silence.

They'd gone nearly a half-mile when Ian stopped. The ranger leaned against a tree and started the painful process of unwrapping a makeshift bandage from around his shoulder. He winced with every twist but kept silent until Regdar caught up.

"Is it following?" the fighter asked.

"How the—*ow!*—bloody hell should I know?" Ian grimaced as he spoke. He'd hastily wrapped more than a few wood splinters into his wound and the bandage was sodden and red. "Sorry," he finally continued. "I don't know, Regdar. You hear anything back there? Ogre's aren't known for being sneaky."

Shaking his head, Regdar looked back into the woods in the general direction of the orc caves. "No. I thought I did, but it must've been an animal. When I stopped, it—"

And then the woods erupted.

How something so large and so violent could come upon the group unawares, Naull couldn't understand. Later, she knew it had to be their fatigue and the creature's knowledge of the area. It came up out of the dell, not along the path but through some secret way, something either the orcs had found or perhaps even prepared in case they'd needed a fast and silent exit from their lair. It had somehow known, or smelled, or guessed, which way the battered party would go, and it roared out of the forest at them.

Early went down first, before he even had a chance to draw his sword. The ogre's club swept around after smashing the big man's shoulder and barely missed Naull as she dived forward onto the ground.

Ian fell next. The half-elf had picked up a stout branch during their retreat, but it snapped when he slashed it against the creature's tough hide. Whirling around, the ogre caught Ian with the horny knuckles of his off-hand and the half-elf flew six feet through the air to crumple against a tree, unconscious. The ogre stumbled over a tree root as it lurched toward the road.

The creature had picked on the softest targets first. As Naull desperately scrambled away on all fours, Regdar drew his bastard sword and screamed in anger at the giant.

"Take this, you mishapen bastard!" the fighter yelled.

The sword split two saplings but didn't slow as it whirled toward its target. Biting into the ogre's tree trunk thigh, it caused the creature to bellow once more in pain and rage. The ogre smashed down with its club, hammering at Regdar's dented armor. He went down on one knee. The ogre, feet planted firmly on the road, raised its weapon for a finishing strike.

The sound of hoofbeats echoed on the path. The ogre whirled toward the south but as the hoofbeats grew closer it saw nothing coming. Across the narrow road Naull lay, speaking a few arcane words and gesturing with components drawn hastily from her pouch.

It wasn't much of a distraction, but it was enough. Regdar caught the ogre's arm as the club came down, then he used the force of the creature's own back-swing to pull himself upright. He stumbled backward, toward the wizard. Screaming in anger, the ogre whirled and came at the pair. It swung its club two-handed, and Regdar readied himself to receive the blow.

Hoofbeats rang out again, this time from the north. The ogre started briefly, then looked down at the wizard and snarled. Naull grinned feebly, still holding the remnants of her spell components, and she pushed herself farther back into the brush. The club reached the apex of its swing, then came down in a killing arc.

From the ogre's chest, a spearpoint blossomed. It was followed immediately by an eruption of red-black blood. The ogre dropped its club in surprise and looked first at Regdar, then at Naull. It tried to twist around but the spear broke and the creature pitched forward just inches shy of Regdar's booted feet.

The two adventurers looked up in wonder. On a gray horse that seemed to shine slightly in the starlight they saw a knight clad in full plate. The knight cast away the broken haft of her spear and raised her mailed hand to her visor.

MANY MEETINGS

The noose snapped the rat's neck. Slowly, the slim line dragged the small corpse over the gravel toward the scrub brush and down past the roots. A scarred, dirty hand grabbed the rat and drew it up. There was a sharp crunch and blood stained the canyon floor.

The rat was Krusk's first food in five days, and its blood his first drink in nearly two. He hadn't wasted time once he reached the cover of the rocks beyond the desert, but the gnolls pursued him as if Hextor's own flails drove them. He'd moved as only a barbarian could, but he was weak with hunger, thirst, and lack of sleep. The gnolls were still relatively fresh and their leader was a masterful tracker.

Krusk's conscious mind didn't consider any of this as he quickly downed the rat, but he was aware of his danger. His heavy brows twitched constantly as he sought the cavern for enemies, but he saw nothing. Still, he felt them. They were out there.

The canyon was coming to an end. After a week's hard march, Captain Tahrain had told him, the canyon would begin to grow more and more shallow and after another day it would end entirely. Rough scrub would give way to low grasses and he should turn west when he came to the first sign of trees. A village lay there. A village was someplace he could get help.

Krusk touched the packet the captain gave him. Not just help, he knew. He needed help that he could trust.

Standing up and flexing his tired legs, he peered back toward the way he'd come.

A week's hard march, his captain had said. Krusk had made the trip in fewer than five days. The barbarian couldn't figure the math, though, and didn't even try. If Tahrain estimated the village lay a little more than a day away from the edge of the canyon, Krusk would reach it before the next nightfall. He thought of the pursuit and knew he'd have to.

Leaving the rat's broken bones and a few bits of hide under the bush, Krusk started off into the growing night.

~~~≫≪~~~

"Grawltak!" The name started out as a rumble in the gnoll's well-muscled throat and ended in a bark. "Captain!" he called out in the common speech.

To a human, it might have sounded like a dog barking, but a gnoll in the center of the canyon looked toward him. Crouching behind a small, scrubby bush, the gnoll waved his paw to attract his leader's attention.

Ten of his gnolls prowled the dark cavern. The darkness of near-midnight didn't trouble them; they sniffed at the ground like dogs and their coal-black, pupil-free eyes made much of the terrain.

The leader, the gnoll with the white patch and the notched ears, sniffed the air and slowly strode over to his subordinate. He approached the small bush warily; he'd had to put down one of his followers already after a trap, set by their prey, broke the fool's leg.

No trap this time, Grawltak thought. He picked at the bones and found the tiny noose. Not for us, anyway.

"The half-orc's hungry," Grawltak pronounced, also in the common tongue.

The younger gnoll seemed to find their quarry's hunger amusing and he cackled. Grawltak cuffed him with the back of his paw but didn't put enough in the slap to make the scout yelp.

"Good work," he growled.

Another, older gnoll joined them. He got down on all fours and sniffed around the bush and the bones.

"No more than four, five hours," he reported.

The old gnoll's speech was almost as clear as any human's, from long practice. The human woman who led them insisted all her servants use the common tongue in her presence, and Grawltak knew the punishments she dealt out to those who disobeyed her. He ordered his pack to speak common all the time so they didn't slip up when she walked among them.

"He's finally slowing down," Grawltak said.

The older gnoll nodded. He reached around his hunched back and drew out a leather bottle. Pouring water from it into a wide cup, he offered it to his chief. Grawltak shook his head and the older gnoll lapped at the water quietly.

"What's out there, Kark?" Grawltak asked.

His voice came harsh as ever, but there was respect there. Most gnolls who reached Kark's age were turned out of the pack, or if they were lucky, killed in a challenge fight. Grawltak saw his old pack leader's value, however, and kept the wise gnoll close.

The younger scout cocked his head and bobbed it obsequiously. The leader growled and the scout stepped back, bowing, then turned to join the others.

"Humans . . ." the older gnoll said as he sniffed the air.

"Close enough to scent?"

"No," the scout barked, almost chuckling. "Not for this old nose, anyway. At least another day's run."

"Then we can catch him."

"It'll be close."

Grawltak bared his teeth and snarled, "If it is, I'll tear some-one's throat out. Get those pups moving, Kark."

The others knew not to tempt their leader's temper. They'd listened, though, and even before the old gnoll jumped toward them, barking, they returned to pack formation and those on the points started forward.

Krusk squinted into the dawn light as he rose up out of the end of the canyon. The fire in his legs matched that on the horizon, he thought, but he continued to ignore it. A stream trickled nearby, and after a quick glance around revealed no signs of danger, the half-orc fell on his chest in the dirt and sank his face into the water.

Guzzling the cool, fresh water, Krusk felt the fatigue in his body start to claim him. He hadn't slept for more than a few min-utes at a time since leaving Tahrain's killers and somehow the lack of water and food kept him from thinking about his exhaus-tion. Now, though, with more water than he could drink and its coolness splashing across his face and neck, he felt his eyelids droop. Rising slowly, painfully to his hands and knees, he cupped the cool liquid into his filthy paws and splashed it into his face.

Krusk sagged by the stream on his knees. His arms hung limply by his sides. Shallow breaths of exhaustion turned to deep inhalations of slumber that nearly drowned out the sound of the riders. By the time Krusk awoke, bleary-eyed and struggling, his greataxe was gone and his arms and legs were bound behind him.

"Are you hurt?"

Naull looked up. The clouds were breaking and she was amazed to see light glinting off the knight's armor.

Dawn already? she thought.

She shook her head and the knight started to dismount.

"No, no," she said, struggling to her feet. "I'm all right."

How long have I been out, she wondered?

Looking around, she judged it couldn't have been long. The ogre's wound still seeped blood and both Early and Ian lay unconscious by the road.

She found herself staring at Regdar, who was staring at their savior—a true "knight in shining armor"—as she stepped away from her horse. The knight was obviously a woman, judging by both her armor and her voice.

As soon as she hit the ground, the knight turned and walked toward Early, who lay by the side of the road. Regdar seemed to snap out of whatever trance he and Naull shared and he hurried after her. The wizard couldn't help but notice how different the two suits of armor seemed—Regdar's was dark, dirty, and dented, while the knight's shone in the sunlight of the new day.

Naull heard Early groan and she followed after the other two. Regdar was in front of the knight and had crouched in front of the big man. Early was sitting up and rubbing his head.

"You all right?" Regdar asked the big man.

"Yeah," Early answered feebly. "What 'bout Ian?"

Early blinked then started, seeing the knight for the first time. His eyes fixed on the knight and didn't leave her as she spun on her heels and strode back across the path toward Ian's unconscious form. Early and Regdar followed slowly but Naull beat them all there. What she saw didn't look good.

The half-elf's shoulder was smashed. His chest rose and fell feebly, but blood from his scalp wound covered his face. Naull bent toward him.

"Don't move him," the knight said from above.

Naull turned back toward the cool, tenor voice. The knight removed her helmet and Naull looked up to see her face for the first time. The woman had black, short hair that stood up at odd angles, as if she cut her own hair with a knife. It should have given her a sloppy appearance, especially since she'd been wearing a full helm only moments before, but somehow it didn't. Her wide, bright eyes met the wizard's briefly, and she crouched by the half-elf's broken body.

"This is bad," the woman said. She opened Ian's light armor and started picking wood splinters from the ranger's wound. The half-elf groaned in pain though he was still unconscious. "He's dying."

It was then Naull noticed something on the woman's breast-plate. Inscribed carefully into the silver armor was a small symbol, an outline of a lightning bolt gripped in a firm hand. The wizard nudged her friend and gestured. He saw it and nodded.

The knight placed both her hands on Ian's wound. She muttered something, but if it was a prayer or a spell, neither friend caught the words.

Ian suddenly moved, arching his back, and he let out what sounded like a startled sigh. The wound on his shoulder closed, and the abrasions he'd suffered seemed completely healed. He opened his eyes and started to sit up.

"No, friend," the knight said, "do not move. You are all right, and among friends, but you are still badly injured."

The half-elf's gaze met the woman's and he blinked in silent wonder. But he recovered his composure quickly and it seemed to Naull almost as if a mask had fallen down across Ian's face. He was back.

"Thank you," he said.

The knight smiled warmly. Her teeth, while white, weren't entirely straight, and that somehow surprised Naull, too. Her ears jutted out, her chin was too large—every individual feature of the knight's face seemed slightly off, but taken as a whole, they somehow added to her attractiveness. She looked at Regdar and the fighter's eyes locked on the woman's face for a few moments. Naull suddenly felt a little uncomfortable and made a sound in her throat. They both turned toward her.

"Yes," the wizard said, "thank you."

Ian lay back against the tree as Regdar and the knight rose.

"I was glad to be of service," she said. "Heironeous be praised, but it seems I got here just soon enough."

Regdar shook his head and chuckled slightly. "Some assistance," the fighter said. He sheathed his bastard sword and looked around. The path looked like a small whirlwind had touched down on it. "You saved us."

He pulled off his right gauntlet and held out a hand, and the woman did the same. The two clasped hands. Regdar's was weather-beaten, scarred, and tanned. The knight's was nearly as large, but pale, and the skin, while slightly freckled, appeared almost flawless otherwise.

Naull shifted uneasily and said, "I'm Naull." She stuck her hand out. "This is Regdar. The half-elf is Ian and the big guy everybody calls Early."

Releasing Regdar's grip smoothly, the knight turned toward the wizard. She continued to smile, as if she hadn't noticed the abruptness of Naull's introduction.

"My name is Alhandra," she replied as she took the wizard's hand in her own. Her grip was gentle but firm. "I am a paladin of Heironeous."

"A paladin," Regdar said with some respect. "I thought as much." He gestured at Ian and back at the horse. It stood over the ogre's corpse, shifting only slightly. "Horse's don't like the smell of blood, or the smell of ogres for that matter, but yours seems remarkably well-trained."

Alhandra strode over to her mount, laughing lightly. She raised her bare hand to the horse's mane and stroked it with obvious love.

"Windlass is a fine mare, aren't you, girl?"

The horse leaned into the paladin's hand and enjoyed the short ear-rub.

"So, um, what brings you here?" Naull asked. "I mean, we're

happy to see you and all, but aren't you a little out of the way? I mean, for a paladin of Heironeous?"

"Naull!"

Regdar's voice had something of a scold to it, and Naull turned and glared at him. If Alhandra noticed the byplay, she gave no sign.

"Word reached me that there was trouble, away south, so I came."

"Trouble?" Naull asked. "Word reached you about a band of orcs raiding trade caravans?"

Regdar gave Naull another warning glance, but the fighter was curious, too.

"No. I hadn't heard about your trouble until I stopped at the town north of these woods."

Naull nodded.

"I decided then to take the woodland path rather than the caravan road, since it seemed the most likely place for the orcs to be."

She said it matter-of-factly, without any hint of a boast, but Naull felt her jaw drop slightly.

"You went hunting a whole orc band alone?" Naull's voice held both disbelief and criticism.

Alhandra nodded and chuckled wryly. "There wasn't anyone else. Still, I'm glad I didn't run into this big fellow alone."

The trio looked at the fallen ogre.

"He was the leader," Regdar said.

"Unusual."

"How so?" Naull asked.

Alhandra shrugged and said, "Ogres are dangerous, but stupid. They don't plan raids; they simply hunt. Of course, I don't know as much about ogres as you probably do...." Her voice trailed off and she shrugged again.

Without a sound, Ian rose up behind Naull and she jumped as he interjected, "No, he had a pair of nasty lieutenants. They probably did most of the planning. The ogre had the muscle."

Ian winced as he tried to rotate his arm.

"We dealt with them, though," Early said. He walked with a limp and used his battered shield almost like a cane. His eyes were dark and ringed with sorrow. "They won't be plannin' any more raids." He looked back up the path, the way they came and asked, "Can we go back, Regdar? For Trebba?"

The fighter nodded.

"Another member of your party?" Alhandra asked gently.

He nodded again and replied, "She killed one of the lieutenants, but died of her wounds. If she hadn't killed him when she did, we wouldn't have made it out alive. Let's go get her."

The party moved slowly through the wood. Alhandra offered her horse first to Early then to Ian, but neither wanted to ride. The paladin brought up the rear, leading Windlass along the narrow path. Naull walked up front with Regdar, and after a while she heard Early tell Alhandra of the ambush and the raid on the orc lair.

Naull grew uncomfortable as she watched the byplay between Early and the paladin. The woman listened to the tale with rapt attention, asking questions as they walked, but the more Early talked the more Naull realized how stupid—and how fortunate—they'd been.

If Alhandra agreed with Naull's assessment, she didn't say so. Indeed, though she commented on their tactics in some very specific ways, she avoided criticizing their efforts. Naull supposed that was for the best. By the time they reached Trebba's body, even Early looked uncomfortable when he discussed their foray into the orcs' lair.

"I am glad the rest of you survived," Alhandra said after they found Trebba's body and loaded it onto Windlass. "It is sad that this one died." Alhandra met Regdar's eyes when she said that and the fighter returned the look stubbornly; it was the paladin who looked away first. "It was a dangerous thing you did."

"And foolish," Regdar said at last.

Naull looked up at him sharply. She felt heat rise in her face.

Who was this paladin to make Regdar say such a thing, even if it was true? But then she looked at Alhandra and saw nothing but compassion on her face.

"That is not for me to say. Who knows what could have happened, or what might have been? You must learn from today and act tomorrow." Alhandra smiled and added, "And that, my friends, is the extent of my philosophy."

They passed a few moments in silence then, staring at the new dawn.

"And your other companion? The dwarf?" Alhandra asked finally.

Ian waved a hand away to the southwest and said, "He's back on the path, between here and the village. We can collect him on the way."

Alhandra started to turn Windlass in that direction and Early moved to follow, but Regdar and Ian stood still.

"What?" Alhandra asked.

Regdar shifted uneasily but Ian remained firm. Looking from one to the other, Naull knew what they were thinking.

I've got to hand it to them, she thought with a mixture of admiration and horror. They're all business.

Naull glanced from Alhandra to Early. The paladin seemed to understand, but said nothing. Early hadn't a clue.

"The treasure." Ian said matter-of-factly. "The orcs' plunder. It's down there," he waved toward the dell. "Let's go get it."

Alhandra said nothing, but Early started turning red. He lurched forward a step, painfully, and jabbed a thick finger at the half-elf.

"You want treasure? After all this? What about Trebba? And Yurgen?"

Ian didn't back down. In fact, he sneered.

"They're dead. So are the orcs," the half-elf said. "Let's get our reward before it's gone."

"The village is paying us. Our reward's there."

Ian huffed, "That pittance? That and the gold I'm getting from the city merchants barely covers my time. I'm here for the orcs' plunder, and I'm going to get it. You want to go back to the village? Fine—more for me."

Early bunched up his fist and took another step forward. Regdar moved to get between them, but before he could, Alhandra spoke quietly.

"Calm," she said simply.

For a moment, Naull wondered if it was a spell, because all three men stopped. Indeed, Early dropped his fist and Ian even seemed to lose some of his haughtiness. Regdar looked back and forth at the two of them.

"That's enough," he added. His voice was firm, but Naull could hear the uncertainty. "Early, nobody's more upset about Trebba and Yurgen than I am. I planned the ambush, and I made the decision to attack the lair—it's my responsibility. Don't be angry with Ian for wanting to do what we all set out to do."

"Reg—" Early started, but the fighter had already turned to Ian.

"Ian, take it easy. You're hurt, Early's hurt, and we're all upset. I know you came here for the reward and the treasure. So did I, but we don't have to forget our friends."

Ian met Regdar's eyes. He didn't nod or say anything, but there was some unspoken acknowledgement.

"We don't all have to go into the lair again," Redgar continued. "Early, if you don't want to, that's fine. You can go with Alhandra." He waited to see if the paladin was willing to submit to his impromptu plan, and she nodded with understanding. "Pick up Yurgen. Ian, Naull, and I will search the lair. If there's anything nasty down there—which I doubt—we'll head back to the village. If not, we'll carry off what we can and stash the rest. We'll meet you along the road. All right?"

No one had any objection. After a short break for a cold breakfast and a mutual checking of bandages, Alhandra and Early made their way back to the path and headed south. Ian led the way back into the lair.

Naull could tell Regdar wasn't as confident about the lair's emptiness as he sounded. Despite the clanking his armor made, he insisted on going in first, with Naull and Ian a good thirty feet behind. But he'd been right. If anything remained in the lair after the ogre left, it had departed soon after.

If any of the three expected large mounds of gold or jewels, they were disappointed. Most of the caravans from the north carried manufactured goods that the orcs either destroyed at the scene or brought back and broke for their amusement.

The orc lieutenants each had decent weapons and armor and some amount of treasure. The trio also found a few rolls of fine silk that the ogre had used for a giant pallet. They could be salvaged, if the soil and stink could be gotten out, but they were too heavy to carry. Almost by accident, Naull discovered a bag under a stone in the ogre's cave. It held nearly all the gold, silver, and jewelry they found in the lair.

"What do you think?" Regdar asked." About a thousand?"

Naull shrugged and said, "You wish. Some of these stones look pretty rough." She held up one large gem in their torch's light. "I'd say seven, eight hundred. Maybe." She tossed it back onto the pile. "I'm no expert, though."

The fighter sighed.

"How about this?" Ian asked, tossing the wizard a small vial. She popped the stopper, dipped a pinky in, and tasted it carefully.

"I'm not sure. It's a potion, but I don't know what it does. Sorry."

The half-elf shrugged. There'd be time enough for detailed examinations later. He gathered up all the decent-looking weapons and armor—not a large amount of either—as well as a ring carved in the shape of a snake. All of it lay on a large, filthy blanket.

"All right; stand back," Naull said.

She gestured and looked at the pile. Not surprisingly, only a few items glowed with the hue of magic. She pointed at them, and the other two separated them from the pile. Concentrating, Naull read them as best she could.

"Sorry, Ian," she said with a grin, "no magic ring."

"So," Regdar said, "three arrows, a dagger, and a bead."

He bent over the smaller pile and picked up the spherical shape.

"Careful with that," Naull cautioned." It's the strongest of the bunch."

"Then you better take it," he said, tossing it to her.

Fumbling with momentary panic, Naull caught the small bead and glared, open-mouthed.

"Regdar!"

"Naull!" he mimicked, then smiled.

She smiled back and put the bead into one of her empty spell pouches.

"If you two are through playing," Ian said, "I'd like to get out of this stink."

Naull wrinkled her nose and said, "Hear, hear."

The party regrouped just outside the edge of the forest. Alhandra's horse was burdened with two corpses, both bundled in old bedrolls and tied carefully on its gray back. Early waved at the trio solemnly as they approached from the woods.

"What is it?" Regdar asked as he jogged toward the road.

Early lifted his arm and pointed south. A thick plume of black smoke rose above the hills.

Regdar cursed. He started to sling the sack he carried over Windlass's saddle, but the horse shied. Alhandra stepped up to him.

"What is it?" the paladin asked. She still had her helmet off, and she squinted toward the smoke.

"The warning fire," Naull said. "Before we went hunting the orcs, we set up a bonfire in the middle of the village. We planted alchemist's fire and some coal dust logs. We told the villagers to light it if there was trouble. Wouldn't help much during the dark, but . . ."

"Sure shows up good in the mornin' light," Early rumbled. He held his sword in one hand and his chipped shield in the other.

"Let's go," Regdar said. "Alhandra, would you . . . ?"

"I beg you to let me accompany you," she interrupted the fighter. He nodded.

"Thanks," Naull said.

The party jogged down the road as quickly as they could. The village lay only two miles south of the treeline, but they had to pass over and around several hills. The smoke grew as they ran and they took that as a hopeful sign—it must have been lit recently. The pile was built to burn fast and smoky, not long.

Ian, even with his wounds, started to outdistance the heavier members of the group, and Naull grew worried he would pass beyond their sight. She'd just made up her mind to sprint ahead and tell him to wait when he halted. As she, Regdar, Early, and Alhandra caught up, they saw a pair of figures, a halfling and a young boy, approaching from the south. They reached Ian at the same time as did the rest of the party.

"You're back!" the boy exclaimed.

Naull recognized him as the innkeeper's son. She couldn't remember the youth's name, though. His father, Eoghan, had done much of the talking for the villagers during their hiring. The boy panted, clutching his side, and the halfling looked at him with grim amusement.

"We came looking for you," said the halfling. His voice had the fine timbre common to his race—not high-pitched or thin, but light and strong.

"Why?" Regdar asked. "What happened?"

"We caught one," the boy gasped before the halfling could answer. His face was flushed, but he obviously wanted to be the one to break the news.

The halfling smiled and said, "The outriders—the ones you

said we should have circling the village—they found one and brought him in. He was exhausted. It looked like he'd had a helluva bad time." There was no sympathy in the halfling's voice.

Regdar nodded, jerked a thumb back toward Windlass and the horse's burden, and said, "So did we."

The halfling paled slightly as he looked up at the two bedrolls and instantly guessed their contents. He looked from one adventurer to another, his gaze pausing briefly on Alhandra.

"Trebba?" he asked. "And the dwarf . . . Yurgen?"

Regdar nodded solemnly and the halfling's eyes dropped.

"What's your name, young man?" Alhandra asked gently but firmly.

"E-Eoghan . . ." he stammered, "but everybody calls me Straw, 'cause Eoghan's my father's name an' I'm in charge of the stable."

"Straw, can you take us to where they have this prisoner?"

"Yes ma'am," he said. "They've got him at ol' Urthar's farm. It's all the way around the village."

"All the way around? To the south?" Naull asked.

"Yeah," the boy answered.

"Why all the way around there?"

"That's where they caught it, I guess," the boy shrugged.

He looked up at Alhandra and she nodded. He started off down the path, with Ian and Early stepping up beside him.

Naull shook her head and yawned. Her head felt like it was full of cotton. Not surprising—they'd all been up for nearly twenty hours. Beneath the dirt and grime, she could see the dark rings under Regdar's eyes and realized she must look pretty ragged herself. She glanced at Alhandra's nearly spotless face and perfect skin, and felt her blood grow a little hot. She turned to the halfling.

"I'm sorry; I don't know you," she said.

"I'm Otto—Otto Farmen." The halfling bowed slightly and added, "I'm a friend of the boy's father. I work with the traders oftimes, but I've been out of town on business."

"Did you see the prisoner?" Naull asked. "The orc the out-riders captured?"

Otto nodded and said, "They sent to the inn right after they caught it. I was just getting up an' Eoghan an' I hustled down to the farm with some others. Eoghan sent me back to light the fire and go looking for you. Straw insisted on coming along."

"Did they really catch it south of the village?" Naull continued.

"Yep. It was down at the edge of the Sandrift, collapsed by one of the springs. Looked like it'd been running all night." He noticed the pair frowning and asked, "Why?"

They told him about their adventures, paying careful attention to their time estimates. Otto took the stories of Yurgan's and Trebba's deaths without comment, but they could see anger smoldering within him.

"So," the halfling said as they concluded their tale, "you don't think this orc is one of the band that's been attacking our traders?"

"Right," Naull answered, and Regdar agreed. "We're certain no others escaped from the ambush, and an orc would not have had time to leave the lair and get all the way around the village before dawn, even if there'd been some reason to do so."

Otto frowned and asked, "So where do you think this orc came from?"

Naull shrugged and Regdar shook his head.

"I guess that's what we'll have to find out," Regdar said. "It bothers me, though."

It bothered Naull, too.

When they reached the village, the square was nearly deserted. One woman stood tending the fire. She waved at them and Straw ran toward her. The party started in her direction then a sound erupted from the south, like a hundred voices all shouting at once. Naull didn't like the sound of it. She turned toward Regdar to say something, but the fighter was already loping across the square. Naull started in surprise to see Alhandra jogging along right beside him.

Another shout reached Naull's ears as they cleared the village square and headed along the south road. The party rounded a corner and headed up a muddy path toward a low ranch house. It looked as if the entire village had walked over the soft earth. A third shout came from behind the barn. They could see parts of the crowd on either side. Some people waved clubs, others torches, and a few had weapons.

"I don't like the look of this," Regdar said.

Naull didn't either, though she didn't know why. If the town truly caught one of the orcs that had been raiding their settlements and trading caravans, they had every right to execute it, though Naull didn't care much for mob rule.

The sight that greeted her when she rounded the corner confirmed her worst fears.

From the hayloft pulley hung a nearly naked body. Streaks of blood ran down the scarred, well-muscled chest and legs. Grayish skin looked almost purple in the morning light. Wounds on the face had closed one eye and the other stared at the crowd dispassionately. As Naull watched, one of the villagers jabbed the hanging figure with a pitchfork. The body twisted and blood seeped out of the wounds as the crowd yelled, but the figure made no sound. It breathed heavily, though, so Naull knew the creature was still alive.

"That's no orc," Ian hissed in her ear.

The wizard gaped. She couldn't imagine how she'd been so blind. The figure twisted back toward her so she could see the face and features clearly. The eyes bulged, the forehead sloped, and one fang protruded from a prominent underbite, but Naull had fought and killed enough orcs to know the difference between those brutal, barbarous humanoids and this poor wretch.

"He's a half-orc," Naull breathed.

"Probably an evil son of a bitch, too," Ian said. Before Naull could object he added, "But he doesn't deserve this. Not just for being in the wrong place at the wrong time."

"Are you sure of that?" Regdar asked. "He could've been up to something."

"Everybody's 'up to something'," Ian answered coldly. He glared at Regdar, then shook his head. "Doesn't mean he had anything to do with our orcs."

"Is it any of our business?" Naull asked, but she knew the answer.

Regdar smirked and said, "Hey, it's not as if we have anything else to do—like sleep." His tanned face was lined with fatigue but also grim resignation.

"How do we stop it?" she asked, looking from Ian to Regdar.

The sharp sound of steel being drawn broke the tired wizard out of her thoughts. She started, seeing Alhandra with her weapon in hand, her silver armor gleaming in the sunlight. The paladin stepped forward. Naull had a horrifying flash of her hacking a path through the unarmored villagers and she put out a hand to stop her.

Regdar grabbed Naull by the arm as she moved toward the paladin. She looked back at the fighter but he shook his head slowly. His dark, tired eyes met hers then looked toward the armored figure striding to the edge of the crowd. Her sword was down and the point moved away from the nearest villagers. Naull's tired mind caught up with what little she knew of Alhandra, and paladins in general, and she relaxed slightly.

As Regdar released his grip on her arm, however, he said, "Be ready." He looked over at Ian, who appeared about to collapse, then he scanned the crowd. "Where's Early?"

Naull shrugged.

The fighter let out an exhausted sigh and said, "Well, be ready to back her up."

The sun shown down on the damp ground and the murmuring crowd, but one thing was obvious despite the dawn: Night wasn't over yet.

THE VILLAGE

"Stop!"

The paladin's powerful tenor cut through the noise of the crowd. Those who saw her stride forward into their midst tugged on their neighbors, who turned and gaped. Others whirled as if struck. No one ignored her cry. Even the prisoner turned his one open eye toward the paladin.

Alhandra stopped halfway through the crowd. Regdar, Naull, and Ian watched uneasily as the men and women of the village closed in around her. Regdar pushed his way forward and the villagers nearest him avoided his spiked armor. Naull fidgeted with her spell pouches, knowing she had nothing left for this sort of situation. She saw Regdar trying to make sure Alhandra had a way out, if she wanted one.

She didn't look like she wanted a way out—or felt she might need one.

"You!" she pointed at the man nearest the rope holding the half-orc aloft. "Cut him down!"

The man actually started forward, but another, bigger man grabbed his arm. The big man held a spiked mace and wore a leather apron around his neck. He hadn't tied it around his back, though, and the apron swung free. Bushy muttonchops covered the sides of his thick face, and his black hair gave him a strong, almost violent appearance.

"No!" the man said.

He didn't exactly brandish his mace at Alhandra, but the challenge was there. Her sword stayed at her side, point down but gleaming naked in the sunlight.

She recognized the big man as Eoghan, the innkeeper. His eyes flickered over the adventurers, particularly Regdar, as his face grew red.

"What's going on? You're supposed to be out huntin' these."

"We were," Regdar shouted in answer. "We did. We got them. All of them," he added pointedly.

Naull wasn't so sure. The figure strung up at the bailing pulley looked very orclike in some ways . . . but not in others. His features, covered in blood and bruises, looked uneven and his skin was grayish, but he didn't have the exaggerated jaw or bushy fur she'd seen so recently on the orc lieutenants.

"Regdar . . ." Naull started.

"Quiet!" Regdar snapped in a whisper, glancing back. "No time for discussion. Shut up and back me up!"

Naull recoiled, stung by his words and surprised at his tone, but the fighter didn't notice.

He shouted to the crowd again, "We ambushed the orcs, followed them back to their lair, and finished them off. None of them escaped."

A ragged cheer went up, but was cut short as Eoghan stamped his foot, drawing everyone's attention back to the prisoner. The crowd murmured.

The paladin, picking up Regdar's cue, said, "Their leader, an ogre, lies dead not five miles north of here, along the forest path. He was the last."

Brandishing his mace like a torch, Eoghan shot back, "Not

the last, knight! I don't know who you are, but we hired them to get rid of all th' scum raiding our farms and killing our friends. All o' them!"

He jerked the rope that held the prisoner aloft. Eoghan echoed Regdar's words in his challenge, but his eyes flashed at Alhandra.

She accepted the challenge. Sheathing her sword with a flourish that showed much practice, the paladin walked slowly toward the barn. Whether grumbling against her or looking awestruck at her, the crowd parted until she reached the bailing porch. She climbed up onto the stand gracefully, despite the bulky armor she wore. Eoghan did not step back, but Alhandra interposed herself between the innkeeper and the hanging half-orc.

"I am a paladin of Heironeous. You know what our order stands for?"

Eoghan didn't respond, but several in the crowd eyed the holy symbol emblazoned on Alhandra's breastplate and looked uneasy.

"Justice," she answered herself. "Law."

Her armor gleamed in the sunlight. Mutters of support began in the crowd, but Eoghan bristled.

"Law? Whose law? Where are you from, paladin?" The big innkeeper slurred the title but Alhandra didn't react. "This is our village. Durandell respects the laws of the king, but no outsider tells us how to enforce our laws!"

He wasn't speaking to Alhandra, but to the villagers. Indeed, Eoghan turned away from the paladin and took half a step toward the crowd. The big innkeeper was used to public speaking. He served as something of a combination mayor and lawyer in the little town. He had the villagers' respect, but he knew an outsider of Alhandra's stature was imposing to the simple village folk. Working to suppress his rustic accent, he wiped his bare hand on his apron and raised it over his head.

"Where were the knights o' the kingdom when the orcs started raiding the few traders we could get to come here, so far off their normal routes?" he asked. "Where were the law keepers when th' orcs raided Tesko's farm?" Eoghan jabbed a meaty index finger at an older man wielding a wooden hayfork. The man had a haunted look in his eyes and nodded grimly. "Where was the soldiery when they burned the Snailrooks' wagons an' killed half the little folk as they tried to escape th' flames?" A plump halfling woman's eyes flashed as several in the crowd turned to look at her. Eoghan whirled on Alhandra and snapped his fingers under her chin. "Where were you, knight? Where were you? When we sent out the call for mercenaries—paid for with what little gold we could raise—*they* came." Eoghan gestured at Regdar and nodded briefly. Then he trained his attention back to the paladin and enunciated his last three words slowly and carefully. "Where were you?"

Alhandra didn't blink, didn't flinch, but she didn't answer, either. Grumbling started again in the crowd.

"She came," Regdar said, stepping forward.

His weapon remained slung across his back, but he stood amongst the crowd in defiance. Regdar presented a stark contrast to Alhandra. Naull supposed the crowd could see just how much mud, blood, and even rust spotted Regdar's plate armor. The goatee and face Naull found dashing hadn't been shaved or washed in days, and dark circles stood out under his eyes. If a few patches of trail dust clung to Alhandra's silver armor and dark traveling cloak, that was all. Naull imagined Regdar looked like a hero the villagers could imagine one of their own becoming, but Alhandra was an alien, an outsider. She was someone who could be held in awe and maybe even respect, but could never be one of them, and Eoghan took advantage of that difference deftly.

But Regdar turned it back on him by supporting the paladin.

"She came," he said again, a little louder. "She came alone when she heard you were in need." He started to walk forward toward Alhandra, but the knight didn't turn. "She traveled miles alone, not for pay, but because she'd heard 'there was trouble away south'—her own words."

Regdar stopped just short of the platform, but didn't climb up to the paladin. He was tall enough that everyone in the crowd could see both of them. He looked her up and down for a moment, the crowd mimicking him, and even Eoghan's eyes followed his.

"We wouldn't be here to hold this debate if it hadn't been for her. An ogre—the orcs' leader—had us dead to rights, when Alhandra, who we'd never met, never talked to, never promised gold," he added with some emphasis, "came riding down and slew him." Regdar threw up his hands. "This woman saved our lives, and stopped the last of the raiders, once and for all. If there's any justice," he concluded, "that, at least, earns her a chance to speak."

With that, Regdar lowered his hands, pausing briefly to put one gauntlet on the edge of the hay porch, near Alhandra's armored foot. She hadn't moved during his speech, but she looked down at his hand, then back up at Eoghan, who still had something to say.

"Regdar," the innkeeper answered with exaggerated care, "no one is questioning your valor or trying to diminish the efforts of you and your companions." He nodded to the fighter and some of the flush started to drain out of his face, but his eyes still flashed and it was obvious he hadn't given up. "If you say this paladin performed valorously in the field, we have no reason to doubt you." He looked around and many heads nodded in agreement. "But—" and he raised his hand, attracting the nodders' attention again—"you are no longer in the field. We caught this orc spying around our southern borders. The outriders that you yourself said we should have on patrol caught him, and we aren't gonna just let him go!" Eoghan's voice rose again, not with anger, but resolve.

"Yes, you are." Alhandra stated matter-of-factly.

She put her hand to the hilt of her sword but didn't draw it. All eyes followed that slight gesture, but Naull realized it wasn't a threat. The sword, as much as the emblem on her chest, was a symbol of her god. She touched it for strength, for support, for divine guidance—or whatever paladins get from their deities.

Naull's tired mind raced. She looked to Regdar but he seemed to be wrestling internally with the same thoughts as her. They'd been hired to protect these people against raiders that turned out to be orcs. Now they were in the position of backing a stranger—albeit a paladin who just happened to have saved their lives—against those self-same villagers.

Then Naull had a thought.

"Alhandra!" she called out. "Paladin!" she cried with emphasis, dashing forward into the crowd.

Faces turned. Eoghan didn't quite turn away from Alhandra, but the paladin herself looked straight at Naull.

"Alhandra," Naull said when she reached Regdar's side. "I know something of paladins and divine magic." Regdar looked at her and cocked an eyebrow. She didn't look at him, but he remembered his own words about backing each other up. "Isn't it true that you can feel—sense—evil?"

Alhandra nodded slowly, and Naull thought she saw a small expression of discomfort on the paladin's face.

"It's true," she said at last.

"So if you examine this prisoner, couldn't you tell us if he's evil or not?"

Alhandra didn't answer immediately. She stood, obviously wrestling with some thought or other but Eoghan didn't wait for her to ponder.

"Is this true, paladin?" he asked. "Can you tell us whether it's a creature of evil?"

"I could," Alhandra said at last.

The crowd seemed to relax. More than a few of the villagers had heard stories of paladins and their holy abilities. Even Eoghan lowered his mace and considered the point. If Alhandra said she could do what Naull suggested, the crowd would obviously like to see it.

But Alhandra didn't relax. She looked up at Eoghan, then slowly turned toward the crowd.

"I could," she declared, her voice grim and cold. "I could examine him and tell you whether the dark taint of evil stains his soul. I could do that for anyone and everyone you brought to me, unless they were protected by powerful magic. I could sit in judgment of anyone you wish. Do you want me to do that?"

Murmuring, the crowd didn't seem to like the sound of that at all. Naull didn't either, but she felt a little betrayed. She'd just offered Alhandra a way out of the mess, and the paladin had rejected it.

"Eoghan . . ." the paladin said to the innkeeper, so gently the man started. "You are a good man. I could tell that were I not a paladin. You and your village have ruled yourselves and worked to obey the laws of the land without hurting others for generations. You don't need me to tell you how to do that, do you?"

The innkeeper stared at the paladin, almost in shock, then he lowered his head and shook it. The loose apron swung stiffly, almost like a wide pendulum, and a deep, rumbling, sardonic chuckle came from the man. He looked up again, an uneven smile on his face.

"Paladin . . . Alhandra, is it?" She nodded back at him. "Y'don't offer easy answers, do ya?"

A few people in the crowd actually laughed.

"The only easy answers are to questions not worth asking," Alhandra said, smiling slightly.

Oh, please, Naull thought, rolling her eyes. But she grinned, too. The crisis seemed over.

"All right, all right," Eoghan said, surrendering. "Cut 'im down!" he called to the guard nearest the hanging figure.

She moved immediately to the prisoner and started to work on the ropes around his wrists. The other guard worked the pulley and lowered the prisoner onto the hay porch.

"Y' don't mind if we ask him some questions, now do ya?" Eoghan asked.

"Of course not," Alhandra agreed, "but he should be treated in a humane manner."

"Well . . . I guess we could put 'im in the inn's root cellar. That's served as a bit of a jail from time to time—but somebody'll have to watch him. I'm not putting him down there with my provender, all alone!"

"I will watch him. I do not say this man is innocent of any crime," Alhandra assured the innkeeper and the crowd, "but he should not be treated as if he is a raider until it can be proven."

Eoghan nodded and stuck his mace in his wide belt. Reaching around, he tied the apron strings behind him. He looked to Naull and Regdar much as he had the night they rode into town. He acted like it too, instructing his guards to place the half-orc in a nearby wagon along with his gear, which lay in a pile nearby, and take him to the inn.

"I'd be feelin' a little safer if you rode along, my lady," he said to Alhandra.

"I will," she said.

"Can you give Ian a ride, too?" Naull asked from below the hay porch. Most of the crowd started back to their homes or nearby farms when Eoghan and Alhandra agreed to terms, and the half-elf looked alone and tired leaning against the fence post. "He's still pretty beat up."

"Still?" Eoghan said, climbing down from the porch.

"Alhandra cured him," Regdar said. "He nearly died."

The innkeeper caught the grim tone of the fighter's voice. He looked around.

"Trebba?" he asked. Regdar shook his head and Eoghan frowned. "And the dwarf, Yurgen?" Regdar shook his head again. "Damn!"

Eoghan stared at the wagon as it rolled away toward Ian with Krusk and Alhandra inside.

"I'm glad I didna' know that before all this. That one might not o' survived to be bickered over!"

"Honestly, Eoghan," Naull interjected, "he couldn't have been part of the raiders' group."

I hope, she added silently.

When they reached the inn proper, Eoghan sent Straw to tend Alhandra's war-horse and both Naull and Regdar helped Alhandra carry their prisoner down into the root cellar.

"He's a big one, isn't he?" Regdar said, huffing a little on the stairs.

The half-orc stood more than six feet tall, Naull could tell as they laid him out on the cellar floor. He had the long, well-muscled but irregular-looking arms common to orcs, but his broad chest and flat features hinted at his human heritage.

It was, however, a slight hint. Naull could see how the villagers mistook him for an orc, especially considering how few of them had ever seen a live orc up close.

"Let's get him cleaned up," Naull said.

Alhandra nodded and fetched a basin of water and a towel from upstairs. When she returned she found Regdar and Naull looking over the half-orc's belongings.

"Find anything interesting?" she asked with intended humor.

Both of them jumped slightly, almost like guilty children. She grinned.

"I didn't think paladins were supposed to have a sense of humor," Naull observed dryly.

Alhandra didn't answer, but an amused smile made the corners of her mouth twitch. She knelt and started cleaning the half-orc's wounds. Surprisingly, he didn't seem badly hurt. A shallow cut across his scalp produced most of the blood. His left eye was swollen but undamaged.

"He's dehydrated. It looks as if he hasn't eaten much in days," the paladin observed finally. "He's out from exhaustion, not wounds."

Regdar yawned.

"He's not the only one," Naull observed. Regdar started to jab her with an elbow but she backed out of the way. "Not with your new armor!" she said, indicating the spikes.

"You two get some sleep," Alhandra said. "I'll look after the prisoner."

Regdar nodded and started up the stairs.

"I'll take these—temporarily," he said, picking up the half-orc's weapons. The rest of his gear lay in a dirty pile on one of the shelves. "Make sure they wake us before they start questioning him, though, all right?"

"I don't think they'll do anything to him now," Alhandra said.

"I just think there's something . . ." But Regdar's mumbling turned to a yawn as he continued up the stairs.

Naull remained behind for a few moments, watching Alhandra clean the half-orc.

"You'll need more water," she said finally.

Alhandra nodded in answer.

"Alhandra," Naull said.

The paladin paused at her labors and looked up. The wizard pushed her bangs back and shook her head against the growing fatigue.

"Even if . . . and I say 'if' . . . this half-orc isn't one of the raiders, who's to say he isn't up to something?"

"Everybody's up to something, Naull," the paladin said, but without amusement.

"You know what I mean. He could still be evil, you know. Maybe a murderer, or a bandit or something. There are some strange things in his gear . . ." Her voice trailed off.

The paladin stood and looked at Naull. Her clear, blue eyes glistened in the dim light of the nearby lanterns as they met the wizard's. Alhandra's simple beauty struck a slight chord of jealousy in the wizard's heart, but she leaned forward, as if confiding in a friend.

"He isn't evil," she whispered.

Naull flushed and asked with a trace and of anger, "Wha—I thought you said you wouldn't use your ability to check him?"

The small smile was back, and Naull felt the flash of anger drain away involuntarily. It was like trying to be angry with a sister, and she'd known the paladin for less than a day!

"I didn't say I wouldn't examine him, only that the villagers should treat him fairly. I looked into his aura the moment I saw him." She looked down at the unconscious half-orc. "I mean," she said in a conspiratorial voice, "wouldn't you?"

Naull didn't know whether to laugh at or smack the paladin, so she did both.

"*Ow!* You're as hard as Regdar!" Naull said. Her anger was gone, and the brief pang of jealousy subsided. "Why didn't you say anything?"

Their eyes met again and Naull nodded.

"All right. I get it," Naull said, then started toward the stairs. "I better get to sleep. When one of you fighter-types can outsmart me, I know I'm tired."

She grinned and Alhandra returned the smile, but Naull paused with one foot on the top stair and leaned down.

"Alhandra, there's one more thing."

"Yes?"

Whispering, Naull asked, "If he had been evil, what would you have done?"

That blue-eyed stare fixed on the wizard's eyes for the third time.

"The same thing," she said.

Naull nodded again and headed for bed.

THE OILSKIN PACKET

The Stag and Stalker Inn had more rooms and better food than most inns in a village this size, Naull allowed. She stripped off her clothing and gave everything but her weapons and component pouches to the innkeeper's wife, a stocky woman with a motherly disposition who went by the nickname "Lexi" and who was willing to do some laundry. After a brief wash in the water basin, Naull flopped down naked on the bed and tried to sleep.

But sleep came slowly, especially considering she, Regdar, and Ian (the latter two shared a room across the hall) had been awake for more than twenty-four hours.

Forget preparing any spells today, she thought, but comforted herself with the knowledge that she shouldn't need any here.

They last stayed at the Stag and Stalker the night before departing to ambush the orcs, and they learned of the trade wagons only an hour before setting out. Now she had a chance to enjoy the room and couldn't do it.

What's wrong with me? she wondered.

Naull thought of the night's events, of the loss of Trebba and Yurgen, and of everything else that happened. It bothered her that she couldn't put it all aside and sleep, despite her grief and sore muscles. That usually meant she was forgetting to attend to something. Sitting up with a sigh, she pulled her pack to the side of the bed and drew out her spellbook.

As long as I'm up, she thought, I may as well review a few things.

Even the methodical study of magic didn't relax her mind. Magic fascinated her, of course, and she'd bought a few new spells before leaving New Koratia. Wizards trained their minds for order and discipline to cast spells. Usually that meant she could fall asleep in moments if she wanted to, just by concentrating.

She wanted to, but she couldn't sleep.

Naull rooted through the rest of her pack. Regdar had the sack of plunder from the orc lair, and there was nothing particularly remarkable in it. She had the bead they found, though, so she looked it over. It was black and hard and she knew it was magical, but it didn't look sinister. She fumbled through the rest of her pack until she found the folded letter from the village leaders, the one that brought them here in the first place.

Something in Naull's mind jumped. She looked at the letter, carefully preserved in an oilskin packet. It never hurt to have the client's own written word when trying to enforce a contract, she knew. She started to open the packet, then she realized that the object on her mind was not the letter, after all. Turning the packet over, she examined it.

Plain. Brown. Slightly rough from wear and long use. Showing signs of much travel. The letter inside was certainly not the first thing this parcel ever contained.

That's it, she thought. The half-orc!

When she and Regdar searched his gear for anything suspicious, they saw a packet tucked into the inside of his chain shirt. She hadn't paid much attention at the time, but she did notice that the packet had some sort of symbol on the side. Naull tried recalling it to her mind. She concentrated.

The sun? she thought, frowning.

Her brow furrowed as she discarded that idea.

A tongue of flame? That was it. It had some sort of fire-symbol on the outside.

She tried to remember what they did with the chain shirt. Regdar had taken the half-orc's weapons back to his room, but the shirt . . . they left the shirt on the shelf in the cellar.

Naull hopped out of bed and strode over to the door. Luckily, she stubbed her bare toe on a chair leg and hopped back, or she would have walked out the door completely naked. For some reason she thought briefly of Alhandra and the attention Regdar had given her.

He'd notice me then, she thought.

She felt herself blush, foolishly. She and Regdar were partners and friends. He'd seen her naked before, and she him. There wasn't much room for modesty on the road, or in a dungeon. Still, her cheeks grew warm as she limped back to the bed.

I'll just wait for my clothes, she thought, lying down. Lexi will bring them, then I'll go get the packet.

She stared at the ceiling, breathing deeply.

An hour later, the door to Naull's room opened a crack and the innkeeper's wife laid the wizard's cloak, breeches, and tunic on the chair without coming inside. She could hear the light snoring and quietly wished the wizard a good day's sleep.

Sides of beef, cured hams, and wheels of cheese hung from the rafters of the stone-lined root cellar beneath the Stag & Stalker. Alhandra saw barrels of wine, spare crocks, and stores common to many inns she'd visited in her travels. The half-orc lying sprawled on the dried rushes spread across the floor, however, was new to her experience. She looked around in the dim light and ran her fingers through her short hair, pulling her headband off and wiping the back of her neck.

"It's all a bit new," she muttered.

Alhandra trained for fighting evil and killing monsters, but she hardly expected her first adventure without a higher member of the order to be so fraught with controversy and intrigue. She was glad she'd met Regdar, Naull, and Ian. They seemed to know what they were doing, and she very much appreciated their support out by the barn. But uncertainty nagged at her, a familiar, if unwelcome friend. She wondered when she'd be rid of it.

She rested on one knee beside the prone half-orc and soaked the headband in the water basin. The two towels she'd brought down were filthy with blood, mud, and dust. She didn't want to bother anyone for more, now that the half-orc was nearly clean. It was obvious he'd spent more than a little time in the desert to the south. Dabbing at the half-orc's wounded eye she saw that it wasn't permanently damaged, but there definitely would be a scar.

Without warning, the half-orc's eyes opened and met hers. For one wild moment she was fascinated. One eye was blue, the other brown. Both bulged in their sockets. One long-nailed hand grasped her wrist firmly while he used the other to prop himself up. She didn't move to resist him.

"Where?" the half-orc growled. His dry throat made his voice crack, but Alhandra couldn't believe it would sound much different otherwise.

"You're safe," the paladin assured him.

The grip on her wrist didn't relax, however, and the half-orc's mismatched eyes stayed locked on her own. Perhaps "safe" wasn't a good enough answer.

"Where?" he repeated. There was no anger or fear in his voice—at least none she could detect—but there was insistence.

Alhandra looked pointedly at his hand, then back at him. She didn't want to give him the idea that he intimidated her. Even though, lying there weaponless and nearly naked, with her wearing her armor and her weapons, he shouldn't.

There's something about him, she thought, but she did not relent.

After a moment, the half-orc released her wrist and used his other hand to rise into a crouch, fluidly, as if there was no effort involved at all. He sat in that crouch easily, but his leg muscles were tense as if he was ready to spring. The paladin moved carefully and slowly, never looking away. She reached for and found a small wooden cup and filled it with water from a pitcher, then offered it to him. The half-orc sniffed at the water before accepting it.

"You're in the cellar of an inn—the Stag and Stalker."

The name obviously meant nothing to the half-orc, but his eyes darted across the walls and the ceiling. Fixing briefly on the stairs, with the door closed at the top and the single, small window with shutters sealed, they came back to Alhandra's face almost immediately.

"The inn is in a small village called Durandell," she continued, watching him.

That got a reaction. The half-orc's bulging eyes widened and he put the cup down. Clear water dripped down his rough chin and onto his gray throat.

"Do you remember what happened to you at the farm?" She didn't like bringing up the subject, but felt it was better to address it now.

The half-orc nodded slightly, but he didn't speak. Alhandra searched his face for some reaction, but he showed none.

Curious, she thought.

"Were you coming here?" she asked.

Shrugging, he picked up the cup again. It was empty. Alhandra broke eye contact and retrieved the pitcher. When she looked back, his eyes were downcast. She filled the cup.

"You're going to have to answer eventually, you know. The villagers don't mean you harm anymore." Alhandra believed that, despite how close things had actually come. "*Evil* humanoids—"

Alhandra stressed the word "evil"— "have been raiding them recently. Orcs, specifically," she added.

Again, the half-orc didn't react. He drank more water, slowly, and when she offered him the pitcher, he accepted it and filled the cup a third time without speaking.

"They want to know where you come from, what you're doing here, and what your intentions are."

When that elicited no response, Alhandra felt her patience wearing thin.

"They'll also want to know who you are."

"Krusk," the half-orc said simply, putting down the pitcher and the empty cup.

He looked at her again, but without the steady concentration of before—no, not at her, she decided, behind her. She looked in the direction of his gaze.

"Ah," she said, rising to her feet. Krusk stayed put, in that uncomfortable-looking crouch. Alhandra took a few steps toward a large ham hanging from the ceiling. She examined it and determined it was thoroughly cured. "I don't suppose Eoghan will mind," she said, drawing out her knife and cutting into the meat, "as long as I pay him for it later."

She sawed off a large chunk of meat, then did the same with a cheese nearby. She looked around and decided that Eoghan didn't keep bread in the cellar. She walked back to Krusk and sat down, handing him the food.

The half-orc attacked it diligently, without a knife. His uneven teeth made short work of the tough ham. Alhandra let him eat, fearing he might choke if she tried to make him talk at the same time. She poured him another cup of water.

As he finished, she said, "Outriders from the village found you, collapsed by a stream. I guess they did this—" she moved her hand toward his bandaged scalp, and he didn't flinch—"but you had more than a few wounds, and you were obviously dehydrated."

"Found a spring," he said.

"You collapsed in it. One of the outriders drove the wagon that brought us here," she added, though he didn't seem to care that she had this information. "You might have died out there, anyway."

A curious expression came over Krusk's ugly face then, but Alhandra couldn't quite interpret it. She decided to probe a little further.

"If you'd been left alone much longer, you would have died, wouldn't you, Krusk?"

The half-orc shrugged but looked defiant. "I survive," he said.

There was a trace of anger there, but Alhandra didn't think it was directed at her, or the outriders who'd found him, or even the villagers who'd tied him up. He made a show, however, of picking up his cup and filling it with water again. She supposed it was his way of trying to change the subject.

"You survived," Alhandra agreed, "but you're stuck here, unless you answer some questions. Eoghan—the innkeeper, the one who agreed to bring you here—he's as much of a leader as this village has. He won't be satisfied with just your name. He'll want to know more."

Krusk started to shake his head, spilling a little water on his chest. He looked down and dabbed at it, then his head jerked up in shock. He started looking around the room wildly and stood up. He narrowly missed smashing his skull on one of the cross-beams in the cellar's ceiling, but didn't seem to notice.

Struggling to her feet, Alhandra asked, "What's wrong? What are you doing, Krusk?"

Dropping the cup, Krusk spun in place. He looked almost comical, examining both himself and his surroundings. The villagers had stripped him down to his torn and stained breeches.

"Where?" he asked finally, looking at Alhandra with fear and pleading in his eyes.

"I told you—" she started, but he shook his head frantically, patting himself with his big hands.

"Where my things?" His voice sounded guttural and his diction almost unintelligible.

He's becoming frantic, she realized.

Alhandra walked quickly to the shelf where Krusk's dirty tunic, patchwork chain shirt, and other gear were piled. He sprang toward her when she lifted it up. Again, he nearly clipped his forehead on a beam, but he ducked as he moved this time.

Krusk grabbed at the chain shirt and Alhandra let him have it, backing away. He tossed it in his hands and something moved.

"Your weapons are upstairs," she offered with a hint of warning.

Shaking his head, Krusk stuck his hand down the front of the chain shirt and came away with an oilskin packet. Emblazoned on the flat side was what looked like a gold and red flame. Krusk dropped the chain shirt immediately and fumbled with the thong on the packet.

Alhandra slowly stepped forward. Krusk looked up and held the packet away slightly, so she stopped moving.

"What is it, Krusk?" she asked in a soothing voice.

He seemed to try to relax, but he didn't put the packet within her reach. When he shook his head, she frowned.

"You're going to have to tell me something, Krusk, or I, or someone else, will have to take it away."

The look that came over Krusk's face nearly made Alhandra reach for her sword. She fought the urge, though, thanking Heironeous that none of the villagers saw the half-orc glare angrily that way. If he'd been awake enough to do that at the barn . . . she drove away the thought.

"I'm just telling you, Krusk. You have to cooperate, at least a little, or there will be trouble. You don't want to have to fight a whole village, do you?"

For a moment the half-orc looked like he might, but then his expression shifted back to its neutral but wary state.

"No," he said.

Alhandra moved back toward the pitcher and away from the

stairs. If Krusk wanted to try to escape, she couldn't offer him a better chance.

Better to find out now, she thought.

But the half-orc rejoined her on the rushes. This time he sat down cross-legged, with the packet in his lap.

"All right, we might as well start with what you were doing at the edge of the canyon—and in the desert before that—and go from there."

Krusk spoke haltingly, and Alhandra knew he didn't tell her everything, but he told her of his flight from Kalpesh, the gnolls, and the death of his friends. The sunlight peeking in through the cracks of the window's shutters faded to amber by the time he finished. The darkness echoed the feelings in Alhandra's heart.

"A whole city sacked, and for—" she stopped.

Krusk had deliberately avoided mentioning anything about the contents of the oilskin packet he still held in his lap, but he had no guile. She knew this Captain Tahrain gave up his life, the lives of his men, and perhaps even the lives of everyone in Kalpesh to keep this packet out of his enemy's hands.

And what an enemy it was.

She shuddered internally, as if someone had poured cold water down her spine. If Krusk had described the marauding commander accurately . . .

"A blackguard," she mused with more than a little irony. "A devotee of Hextor."

She shook her head and looked away, thinking of her trainers, her mentor, and the fact that this was her first quest away from the guiding arms of the Order of Heironeous.

Well, they never said the life of a paladin would be a dull one, she thought wryly. Or long, for that matter.

FIRE IN THE NIGHT

"I'm certain, captain," the young gnoll whined. "They brought the half-orc here."

Grawltak stared at the rutted, muddy field. When they tracked their quarry out of the canyon to the spring, he nearly tore the throats out of his young scouts. Kark intervened, however, pointing out that while they couldn't pick up the half-orc's scent after that, the hoof prints clearly led north. Someone picked up their prey and carried it away.

"I don't understand . . ." Grawltak mused aloud.

The young scout didn't dare speak, but the old lieutenant, Kark, did.

"The blood we found near the spring. We thought we hurt the half-orc. They found and captured it and brought it here."

The gnoll leader thought about this then barked in laughter as he thought of the irony. He'd nearly panicked because he thought someone helped his quarry to escape. The torn-up field and the wagon tracks, the blood they could all smell near the barn, all pointed to the same thing. No one rescued the barbarian—it was captured. When Grawltak's soft barking threatened to turn into a howl of relief, however, the gnoll felt Kark's claws touch his arm.

Light came from the farmhouse. They waited until dark to come close to the settlement, and they watched from the hedgerow.

"What now, pack-master?" the young scout asked.

Grawltak stared at him. "You, and you—" the gnoll leader pointed at another of the pups—"go search the barn. Find out if they killed it."

The chosen pair looked uneasy.

"The animals . . ." one said.

Baring his teeth, Grawltak snarled. Animals, particularly farm-raised fowl and pigs, didn't like gnolls at all. They tended to make a lot of noise if they caught the scent of gnoll hunters. On any other occasion they'd be right to fear the gnoll pack. Tonight, Grawltak didn't have time to raid.

"Be certain they don't smell you, idiots!"

The wind blew from the west. It wouldn't take much time for his scouts to circle around and come in from the . . . Grawltak cursed violently. All the other gnolls nearby flattened their ears and cowered, except Kark, who nodded. To the east of the barn lay the farmhouse.

Grawltak sneered at his lieutenant and growled, "Take three more of these fools up to the farmhouse. If anyone notices anything, kill everyone. No one escapes!"

His pack, even Kark, nodded and yipped, eager to please. They'd better be. When the barbarian escaped them in the desert, Grawltak had seen death in his mistress's eyes. He was still surprised she'd punished only one of his pack, but she was in a hurry. She took the shamans after they questioned the dead—Grawltak's fur stood on edge as he remembered that—and they'd had little contact with her since. The gnoll fingered the amulet he wore and wondered if he should report in again.

No, he thought, the next time I see the mistress, the half-orc's blood will be in my mouth. I'll show her his torn throat and she will be pleased.

Despite his pack's fear of discovery, the scouting went well. None of the human farmers came out, even when one of the chickens got out of the coop and Kark snapped its neck.

"If they killed the half-orc," the scouts reported, "they didn't do it here, pack-master."

"Where is it, then?"

Wagon tracks rutted the ground and led north, toward the village.

"The ground was soft, pack-master. We can follow the tracks easily."

"Do it," Grawltak replied. Dark covered the land but the night was clear. Starlight and the sickle moon made it easy for the gnolls to see, but they could be seen, too. "Stay low and near cover."

Crouching and loping in pairs, the party of gnolls moved silently toward the village. No one marked their passing.

No one noticed the gnolls on their way from the farm because everyone not in their homes was stuffed into the Stag and Stalker's common room. Eoghan made sure everyone had something to drink—but not too much—and a few things to eat, then he took off his leather apron, handed it to his wife, and opened the cellar door.

Naull looked on from a seat near the hearth. No fire burned. She supposed they only used the fireplace on cold winter nights and those came few and far between in Durandell. Regdar sat across from her, wearing his newly-cleaned and repaired armor. She wondered why the fighter wore it now, but she didn't ask.

Ian came down from his room just as Alhandra stepped up

from the root cellar. Naull looked at her in surprise. Was she down there this whole time? The paladin still wore her armor and had her sword at her side.

I guess so, Naull thought.

Ian pulled up a stool next to Naull and leaned over.

"Sleep well?" he asked.

She nodded, even though she'd had some pretty bizarre dreams. Naull didn't believe in precognition—well, except as a deliberate spell effect, of course—but she still felt uneasy.

Murmurs started as the half-orc followed Alhandra up out of the cellar. Most of the villagers were at the farm earlier, when they saw him strung up, bloody, and exhausted.

Alhandra's been busy, Naull thought. She even found him a shirt.

It was a tattered white tunic and it barely stretched across the half-orc's massive chest. He still wore his short breeches, but it looked like either he or Alhandra cleaned off most of the dirt.

At Eoghan's direction, Alhandra and Krusk moved to one of the shorter tables nearby. It stood close to the hearth but far away from any of the exits. It didn't appear to be an effort to keep the half-orc from escaping; placing him in that spot just made it easier for everyone to see him without shifting around much.

Naull and Regdar scanned the crowd but Ian watched the half-orc. He sat uneasily on a chair by the table. Alhandra whispered something to him and he seemed to relax slightly. One hand hovered near his chest.

"Regdar?"

Naull nudged her partner and he turned to face her.

"What?" he whispered.

"Has he got something there?"

Regdar squinted, though they weren't more than a dozen feet from the half-orc.

"I don't know," Regdar answered. "His stuff's over there."

He pointed to a basket containing a small pack and the half-orc's chain mail. Someone had brought it up from the cellar. Regdar propped up the barbarian's axe and bow in the corner nearest his seat.

Opening her mouth, Naull started to say something, but Eoghan thumped a block of wood on the table. He, Alhandra, and the half-orc all sat behind it. Everyone else in the inn found a seat or a post to lean on and the room grew quiet.

"This is not a trial!" Eoghan said in a loud voice. "Our ... visitor hasn't done anything to be put on trial for." The innkeeper nodded along the table at the half-orc, who didn't appear to notice. Alhandra, however, inclined her head in thanks. "But we have a responsibility t'know who he is an' what he's doin' here."

Alhandra stood. "I will speak for this man," she said in a clear voice. "He answered my questions, and though I am not of your village and have no authority here, I am satisfied he means no harm and has done nothing that would threaten Durandell or any of its interests."

A few hours ago, Alhandra won over a hostile crowd on the verge of lynching the half-orc. Naull and Regdar exchanged glances and looked over the villagers in attendance. A few nodded already, as if that was good enough for them.

Okay, I'm impressed, Naull thought.

The hearing went well and quickly, though there were some incidents of interest. When Krusk—as Alhandra introduced him—told haltingly of the attack on Kalpesh and its likely fall to an army of humanoids, many of the villagers cried out in dismay. Because of the desert and the dangers of the canyon in between, Durandell had little contact with the southern city. Every so often, however, a traveler did come through, bringing stories of the exotic desert metropolis, silks, oils, and other goods not often seen in the small town. One of the inn's favorite decorations was an oddly-shaped oil lamp that hung above the fireplace. It had a foreign appearance with its long neck and more than a few villagers looked up at it when they heard of the storming of the city.

No one asked how or why Krusk and a few other men and women from the city escaped. All assumed those refugees fled in fear of their lives, or perhaps in a desperate but doomed effort to find help. Ian frowned, however, and Naull exchanged a look with the half-elf. They both met Alhandra's eyes as she helped Krusk relate the story of the battle at the edge of the desert. Naull almost let out an audible gasp when she saw the paladin shake her head, almost imperceptibly, as their eyes met. The two locked gazes until Naull shut her mouth and nodded slowly.

There's more to this, she thought. She turned to Regdar to tell him, but then several things happened at once.

Crockery smashed against the floor as the innkeeper's wife Lexi looked up and screamed. She'd been moving through the crowd with a jug of small beer, refilling cups as needed when, with a crash of glass and fire, a lantern smashed through one of the windows on the front wall of the inn. Glass and oil splattered across two villagers and a ball of flame erupted on the hardwood floor. A flaming arrow shot through the open door of the inn, narrowly missing a tall man in a fur tunic. It struck the far wall above the bar and kept burning.

The villagers cried out in fear, shock, and in a few cases, pain. Everyone started moving at once. A few jumped behind the bar, others tried to scramble away from the fire, some even bolted toward the door.

"Stay inside!" Regdar shouted to those few.

He started jumping in that direction, but Early, who had entered the inn only a few moments before, got in his way.

Two more fiery arrows shot through the door. One hit the far wall and snapped. The other embedded itself in a villager's chest. She had just stepped into the center of the doorway, meaning to dash out into the darkness. Instead, she collapsed backward, a look of shock on her face. The flame on the arrow shaft sputtered and died, drowned in blood oozing up from the wound.

"Get down!" Regdar shouted.

He turned to Eoghan. The innkeeper's look of anguish and confusion showed he might have some experience settling disputes and leading his neighbors, but none in battle.

"Get down!" Regdar repeated. "Flip up that table and get behind it!"

Eoghan obeyed and Alhandra helped him push over the table into a barricade. Other villagers did the same with other tables. Ian leaped to the side of the smashed window, slamming the inside shutters closed. An arrow, this time unlit, smashed through a crack in the wood bare inches from his hand while he fumbled with the bar. Another villager went down with an arrow in his thigh, but he managed to push the inn's door closed with his shoulder.

"Upstairs!" Naull cried.

Too many people were packed into one room. If their unknown attackers threw in more oil, someone else would die.

There was a stampede for the stairs, and a few of the smaller folk were nearly trampled. Early scooped up a halfling man and helped him to the stairs.

"Who are they? What do they want?" Eoghan panted from behind the upturned table.

His wife, who had scrambled behind the bar after dropping her tray and collapsing, made her way to his side. Both husband and wife looked pale and shaken.

Regdar shook his head and took stock of the room. Nearly all the villagers were upstairs, spread through the rooms. He saw Ian crouching by the closed window and swore.

"The window in our room! Ian, it's open."

The half-elf nodded and said, "I need to get my weapons, anyway."

He looked over at Naull and headed toward the stairs.

"What the hell do you think you're doing?"

Early's shout made Ian stop at the base of the stairs, but Regdar signaled for him to keep going.

The cry was directed at Krusk, who was moving toward his weapons and armor. The half-orc didn't even pause as Early moved toward him. Alhandra tried to step between them but the big man raised his sword threateningly.

"He's still a prisoner, isn't he?" Early shouted. The big man looked grim.

Krusk yanked his chain shirt down over his chest but Early put a hand out when the half-orc reached for his axe. Krusk's right hand balled into a fist.

"Stop it!" Naull cried out.

They both looked at her.

"We don't have time for this," the wizard said. She turned to Regdar and asked, "What do we do, boss?"

For a moment, Regdar looked flustered, then he shook his head and pointed to the innkeeper.

"Eoghan," he said, "get every container you can find filled with water. Is the back door locked?"

Eoghan shook his head in shock, but stood up. He started toward the back, then stopped and turned.

"I'll get it, dear," Lexi said, almost as if she was talking about a pie in the oven, then she struggled to her feet and hustled toward the back of the inn.

Eoghan nodded and began handing out jugs and pitchers to the few villagers who still remained on the ground floor.

"Get some of the water upstairs. Thank Pelor the roof isn't thatched," the innkeeper said. He knew the wood slats would burn quickly if more flaming oil went up there, but they could only do their best. With a puzzled look on his face, he turned toward Naull and asked, "Why've they stopped?"

It was true. No more arrows thunked against the door or the walls. They still heard howling outside, but that was all.

"I don't know," she answered.

After seeing to it that Early moved away to help one of the fallen villagers, she'd helped Krusk get into the rest of his armor.

"They want me," Krusk said.

His axe balanced deftly in his big hands and a dark expression clouded his face. He moved toward the door. Nearly everyone stepped out of his way, but Alhandra intercepted him.

"No, Krusk, you can't."

"No more running," the half-orc rumbled.

The paladin started to argue, but a loud baying from outside the inn cut her off. It was loudest just outside the front door, but answering yelps and howls seemed to echo from all around. Then it all stopped, suddenly.

"Come out, half-orc!" a canine voice howled from in front of the inn. It sounded almost like more baying, but the words were clear. "Come out and give us what we want! Come out, or we'll burn you out, you and your new friends!"

Barking laughter rose again, and through the slits of the shutters and cracks of the door they could see many small fires in the courtyard. Torches, lanterns, all moving, all dancing just beyond the wooden walls of the inn.

FLIGHT

"Send him out!" the howling voice continued. "We only want the half-orc! We don't need to roast all of you in your little wood oven!"

Barking laughter followed.

"I don't think he means it," Naull said grimly.

"What?" Eoghan asked anxiously. "Whatever that is, it'll burn my whole place down!"

Regdar turned to the near-frantic innkeeper and said, "That's not what she meant. Whatever that is, it'll burn this place down whether we send Krusk out or not."

The half-orc paused in his tracks. He was halfway to the door, but Regdar's words stopped him.

"Yes," the barbarian growled, almost to himself. "They burned Kalpesh . . . they'll burn here as well."

"Then what can we do?" the innkeeper almost wailed.

The look on the fighter's face told Naull he was wrestling with that question already. Regdar shook his head and moved to the door, peering carefully through one of the cracks. Something thudded into the wood and he leaped back.

"I can't see them; it's too dark. I don't know who they are."

"They're gnolls."

The assemblage turned and looked at the stairs. It was Ian. Soot stained his bandaged arm. Their attackers had fired flaming arrows into the top floor, too, but the half-elf and the villagers extinguished the small blazes.

"I saw them through your window, before we shut it. There's at least a dozen of them, maybe more. They all have bows and torches. They've dragged a couple of hay bales from the stable out into the courtyard and set them aflame."

Regdar cursed.

"At least they haven't set the inn on fire, yet," Naull observed hopefully.

A few of the others nodded, but Regdar frowned.

"Why not?" he asked. "I mean, with us yelling and arguing in here, they could've soaked the walls with oil and put a torch to us all. Instead they launch a few fire arrows and this—" he pointed to the scorch mark and the smashed lantern. "What did they do upstairs?"

"A couple of arrows. One caught on your bedding," Ian shrugged. He understood where Regdar was headed. "We put it out with the water from the basin. No problem."

"So, they don't actually want to burn us out. They want Krusk," he nodded at the half-orc. "But they want something else. Otherwise, they'd just fire the inn and catch him when we ran for it. Whatever they want, it's something they can't get if they burn the inn to the ground."

Alhandra looked deliberately at Krusk, who returned her gaze and shook his head. Naull caught the interplay, as did Regdar. Ian actually stepped toward the half-orc, but he put up his hand up when Krusk growled and raised his axe.

"Krusk, no," Alhandra said. "You have to tell them. No one here wants to hurt you, but they have to know."

For a moment the half-orc looked defiant, but then his face collapsed into sorrow, then acceptance. It amazed Naull to see how expressive he was. When he looked defiant or angry, he looked most like the orcs they'd fought and killed, but now he just looked like a sad, ugly man.

Reaching into his chain shirt with one thick hand, he drew out an oilskin packet. Naull nearly smacked her forehead as she recognized the flame symbol on the outside. She had meant to ask Krusk about it when things settled down, but they never did.

Whatever it was, the half-orc valued it highly. When Ian leaned in to get a closer look, the half-orc started to move the packet away protectively, but at a word from Alhandra he stopped and held it up.

Without the flame emblem it would have looked almost exactly like the packet in which Naull kept her important papers, such as their contract with the village. It was a little bulkier, as if a few more things were stuffed into it, but otherwise the same size and shape.

"What's in it?" she asked.

Alhandra started to answer, but Krusk shook his head brusquely.

"It's what Kalpesh . . . and my friend," he said haltingly, "died for. They can't have it. No one can have it. I must protect it."

"Why? If they were willin' to burn down a whole city," Eoghan suddenly cried, "they'll sure as the Nine Hells burn us alive for it!" Lexi, back from securing the rear door, tried to restrain her husband. He shook her off and continued, "What's so important? Why can't we jus' give it to 'em, so they'll go away?"

Krusk's jaw jutted out as he turned to face the big innkeeper, but he didn't answer immediately. He looked at Alhandra, but she made no move. Naull watched as the half-orc's jaw worked and she felt she saw him come to a decision.

They locked gazes for a moment. Krusk's bulging eyes blinked, and he nodded.

"The City of Fire," he said in a low, rough tone. "The key."

Only those standing immediately around Krusk—Alhandra, Naull, Ian, Regdar, and Eoghan—heard what the half-orc said. The rest of the inn's occupants, only a few feet away, heard the howling of the gnolls outside and their own frightened voices.

Even Early didn't hear Krusk continue in a low voice, "The captain gave this to me to protect. He wanted me to find help and go to the City of Fire before . . ."

Krusk's voice rasped to a halt, and he looked at their faces again. Trust came hard to the rough outcast, Naull could see. Here he was trying to make a leap of faith with people who, only hours earlier, had nearly lynched him. Naull couldn't imagine what he was experiencing, but she found herself respecting him, and Alhandra as well. Clearly the paladin had connected with the half-orc on some level during their time in the cellar.

"Before she gets it," Krusk finished.

"She?" Regdar asked. "Who is she?"

"A blackguard," Alhandra answered. "He told me. A blackguard of Hextor seeks the key. The gnolls are her creatures."

Eoghan blanched and turned away. It was too much information for the innkeeper to handle. Ian let out a light whistle, but Regdar frowned.

"The City of Fire?" he asked. "I've never heard of it."

Naull reached out and stroked the packet and the flaming symbol. There was something there, she thought, in the back of her mind. Then it clicked. Ancient texts from her apprentice studies came back in a rush and she remembered.

"The City of Fire . . . I know about this. Krusk, did your friend the captain tell you any other names? Did you hear him say, 'Secrustia Nar,' or did he call it 'the Flamestar of the Desert'?"

The half-orc's eyes widened, and he nodded.

"Se-Secrustia Nar," he pronounced haltingly. "City of Fire's ancient name."

Naull looked around the small group in surprise at the half-orc's pronouncement.

"Don't tell me you've never heard of Secrustia Nar?" The name had Draconic origins, and the stories and legends flooded back. "Don't any of you ever read?"

Alhandra appeared concerned, Ian annoyed, and Regdar

amused. Naull looked back at Krusk last and she sobered at his expression.

No, I don't suppose you do, she thought.

Amusement waned quickly for Regdar, however. "Okay, Naull—you're smarter than all of us," he said. "How about letting us in on the joke before the gnolls get impatient."

The gnoll commander, if that's what it was, was shouting again for Krusk to be sent out. More threats and flaming arrows would not be far behind.

"Oh, it's no joke," Naull replied. "It's a legend, and one I don't have time to go into. Do you know the story, Krusk?"

The half-orc gave something of a nodding shrug.

"I only know enough to understand why Krusk doesn't want to give up that packet," Naull continued, "and why we shouldn't, either. Regdar, the City of Fire is ancient. I've heard the earliest settlements around Kalpesh were just traders' way-stations when Secrustia Nar disappeared. It is, or was, one of the oldest cities in this part of the world. It makes sense, I guess, that the key would come to Kalpesh, though," she mused, but then she shook her head. This was no time for history lessons.

"The City of Fire was supposedly a link to another plane. You've heard me talk about other planes, right?"

"Sure," Regdar said. "The Outlands, the Big Ring—"

"The Great Ring," she corrected.

"Right. The elemental planes—"

"Yes!" Naull exclaimed. "The City of Fire, according to everything I've read about it, had a link to the Elemental Plane of Fire. A permanent one, not something like the temporary ones powerful wizards or clerics sometimes set up."

Alhandra looked grim, but Regdar still needed further explanation.

"According to legend," Naull continued, "Secrustia Nar stood between the Elemental Plane of Fire and our plane. Some people call these sorts of places 'pocket dimensions,' but it doesn't matter.

What does matter is that the people who lived there were able to command and control incredible elemental forces. They had servants and even armies of fiery beings, and they supposedly dominated this whole part of the world. There are even legends that say Secrustia Nar is why we have a great desert here instead of fertile lands." Her voice grew ominous. "When the City of Fire's rulers couldn't control their servants anymore, the Elemental Plane of Fire swallowed it up, burning the lands around it."

Regdar whistled. "And this key?"

Naull nodded to Krusk, who was listening intently to her story. He added nothing, but she thought she saw him nod once or twice.

"Supposedly," she said, catching Krusk's glance and holding it, "a few of Secrustia Nar's people escaped the disaster. They made a map that told the way back to where the city's primary planar gate once stood, and they kept a key to safely open that gate. Most of the stories say wise clerics of Pelor and Heironeous destroyed the map and hid the key, but I guess that's not the case, is it, Krusk?"

Shaking his head, the half-orc slowly opened the packet. He fumbled inside for a moment, then drew out a strange-looking golden disk. It was shaped like a ball of fire, but flat. As he held it in his gray palm, it glowed slightly, and the carved flames on its outer edge flickered in different colors, from gold to red, then orange and other colors of fire.

"My captain made me memorize the directions to the city. I can find it. I can open the gate with this key, and I can close it forever," he said, finally. The half-orc closed his fist over the flaming disk and looked at each person in the group in turn. "I will do this. I have sworn it."

"I think that's a pretty good idea," Naull agreed.

"No," Regdar disagreed. "Why not just destroy it? Burn the papers and smash the key?"

Naull shook her head. "All the legends—all the stories that talk about destroying the key—say that it isn't easy. Some say the key has been destroyed, several times, but it keeps reforming. Like fire that you put out in one place, only to have it rekindle in another."

"I must close the gate," Krusk said simply.

Something struck the inn's door. This time it was not an arrow, but something heavy. They heard running footsteps retreating down the stairs and away into the courtyard.

"Open your doors!" the gnoll leader howled. "We won't attack, yet! See what is in store for you!"

At Regdar's direction, Early and Alhandra moved to either side of the door. Regdar took up a position directly in front of the door, holding Alhandra's shield before him. At his nod, they opened the door. Something propped against it fell inside. Regdar looked down and saw a burned and bloody corpse.

"Take him in! Look at him! It's what we will do to every villager we find unless you send out the half-orc!" bayed the gnolls' leader. "Send him out! Or look upon your own deaths!"

The pack howled in unison at the threat.

Regdar glared into the darkness, then used his heavy boot to push the corpse out of the door. For a brief moment the jeers of the gnolls stopped. The corpse turned over and rolled down the porch stairs. The gnolls howled again, this time in anger that their taunts hadn't succeeded.

"Vernon . . ." the innkeeper gasped. He'd watched Regdar from behind the door. "The blacksmith . . . oh, gods! How could you—"

Eoghan's accusatory tone cut off as Regdar turned toward him, glaring with anger.

"He's dead," Regdar said flatly. "We can't help him, and his corpse is no use to us. We've got to figure a way out of this. Then you can mourn him," the fighter added a little more softly.

Eoghan nodded and deflated slightly.

"I'm going out there!" Early shouted. "We can fight them!"

"You wouldn't get near them," Alhandra said. "They all have bows, and we can barely see them."

"I can see them," Ian said, but he didn't look happy about the idea.

"I can, too," Krusk added. Early looked at the half-orc in surprise. "No more running. I fight."

Early nodded slowly and said, "All right, then! Let's go."

"No," Regdar said. He still stood near the closed door, and he barred their path. "This isn't the way."

Alhandra stepped up to support the fighter, and Naull edged around to one side.

"Then what is the way?" Early asked angrily. "Do you have another plan?"

Regdar didn't answer immediately.

"Are you so eager to die, Early?" Naull asked sarcastically.

Early whirled toward her with a snarl but Alhandra stepped between them.

"Don't be a fool," she said. Her tone made Early stop and gape. "Listen. Think."

The two words seemed to cut the anger out of him, and he fell silent.

After a few long moments, Regdar spoke again, this time loud enough for everyone on the main floor of the inn to hear.

"If we go out there and fight," Regdar said slowly, "we could win. We might kill all the gnolls before they kill all of us."

The fighter let the double impact of that statement sink in. The few villagers still downstairs exchanged uncomfortable glances. Ian shrugged, but he hadn't moved toward the door to support either side.

"But if we don't," Regdar continued, "if they kill all of us instead of just some of us, they'll take a prize back to their leader. A dangerous prize."

He looked over at Krusk. The half-orc looked uncomfortable, but Regdar knew he couldn't sway anyone to the right course of action without giving some reason for it.

"We do believe that the gnolls attacking your village are after one thing. When that thing leaves, they must follow it, and you'll be safe." Some of the villagers muttered uncertainly, but Regdar kept on, "We can take this thing and try to escape with it, but I know that's asking a lot of you. How do you know you aren't just helping us to escape, with you remaining behind to die in the fire?"

More muttering started. Naull shifted uncomfortably but remained silent.

"I have no answer for that," Regdar concluded. "You'll have to trust us."

He looked over at Alhandra, standing tall in her shining armor, then he turned to Krusk. He met the half-orc's eyes and the barbarian nodded, as if Regdar was talking to him, not the villagers.

"I trust you," Ian said. "I'll stay. I can't ride with this, anyway," he said, indicating his bandaged shoulder.

The half-elf looked at Early. The big man's face showed his emotions clearly. He felt anger, pain, and fear, but resolution slowly formed. He stepped over to Ian and held out a large hand. The half-elf took it in his own small grip and pumped it once.

"Me, too," Early said. "This is my village, and I trust you, Regdar." Quietly, he added, "I hope you know what you're doing."

"Me, too," Regdar replied in a low voice. "Here's my plan," he said, gesturing everyone to draw near.

Naull somehow grinned even as the gnolls' howling increased.

"What's taking so long?" Grawltak barked at Kark.

The older gnoll rounded up two more hapless villagers, a human girl and an old dwarf. They'd already burned the dwarf's beard away—gnolls hated dwarves as much as any of the "civilized" peoples—but they stopped short of killing him.

Maybe I'll use one of my mistress's favorite tortures, Grawltak thought, eying a wagon wheel and thinking of his black-armored leader. Crucifixion seems to impress the soft-skins.

He was about to order the girl stripped and tied to the wagon wheel when the door to the inn flew open. In it, behind what looked like half a broken table, stood a hulking figure. The dim light posed no problem for the gnoll's eyes, however. He saw clearly who it was, and he panted in pleasure.

"So, half-orc, you're coming out at last! I hope you still have what I've come so far to get! My mistress will be displeased if you've lost it."

From behind the table-shield, Krusk raised one hand and showed the oilskin packet. He took a step out of the doorway then stopped. A few of the gnolls moved forward, but he leaned back.

"Well, come on, half-orc!" Grawltak shouted. "What are you waiting for? Your friends have decided your fate. Come forward quickly, or I'll add this one's blood to the night's pool!"

Kark passed the human girl to Grawltak, and she sobbed as he threw her roughly to the ground.

"Let them go!" the half-orc called back, half question, half demand.

Hyenalike laughter answered him, but Grawltak stepped forward and barked for silence.

"Of course! They mean nothing to us. My mistress is impatient! I will not take my pleasures in this village if you surrender yourself. Who knows? If you cooperate, maybe you, too, will live. I don't blame you for trying to survive!"

Grawltak looked around the courtyard. He tried not to glance too long in the direction of the gnolls positioned closest to the inn. Each had two bottles of alchemist's fire. When they had the half-orc in tow and knew the burden he carried was theirs, they would splash the inn. The burning and the death would keep the soft-skins from pursuing.

"We'll take your weapons, but even those you might get back, if you cooperate!"

No barks of laughter answered Grawltak then. He could feel the tension in his pack. They were waiting for the kill.

The half-orc stepped forward. He kept the table in front of him as he moved across the porch, down the steps, and onto the courtyard grass. A few of the gnolls stepped forward into the light of the burning hay bales. Grawltak himself moved forward, with Kark beside him, but something made him pause.

It saved his life. The shutters of the upper story of the inn flew open and arrows shot out. Two struck the ground inches away from Grawltak's feet and others hit each of the gnolls moving toward Krusk. One of those gnolls collapsed with a howl, but the other pulled the shaft out of his leather armor and leaped forward, axe in hand.

The half-orc threw the table at the gnoll, and the unexpected attack caught the creature off-guard. As the humanoid leaped aside, Krusk swept out his own greataxe and brought it smashing down against the gnoll's shoulder. Swinging back, the whining creature managed a weak blow against Krusk's side.

The rest of the gnolls reacted quickly. Kark's archers loosed their arrows at the half-orc, but Krusk was partly shielded by the gnoll in front of him. Only one arrow struck its target, and it thudded harmlessly off the half-orc's chain shirt.

Grawltak howled in anger. The gnolls heard him and those with the alchemist's fire jumped out from their cover and made ready to throw.

As they waited for Grawltak's signal, the stable door exploded outward. A human woman in gleaming armor rode right over one of the fire-flask gnolls as she spurred her horse forward. Another rider followed her, this one a human man. His armor was darker and covered in spikes. Grawltak swept out his axe and with Kark at his side, charged to meet them.

But the soft-skins weren't yet out of surprises. Roaring out of the inn came three more humans. Three large men wielding motley weapons bore down on the gnolls. One buried a scythe in the head of the gnoll nearest Krusk while another threw himself at the second flask-carrier. The alchemist's fire fell from the startled gnoll's hands and exploded on the ground.

One gnoll remained poised to throw fire onto the inn's roof.

He threw it without waiting for Grawltak's bark, and it caught quickly. The right side of the inn's roof blazed.

Cursing, Grawltak snapped more orders reflexively, this time in his native tongue. He could not shout as loudly or as quickly in the awkward common speech, and he was too angry for that anyway. More gnolls dashed forward from their hiding places. Some fired flaming arrows at the inn while others attacked the soft-skins in the courtyard.

The riders didn't let the gnolls turn the tide against them that easily. The shining knight swept out her sword and hacked down the gnoll nearest her, then she spun her mount toward the next one, who was wrestling with a human on the ground. The gnoll rolled away from its big opponent in fear of the horse's hooves, and the knight just missed decapitating it with a sweeping blow. The gnoll yelped in pain as the sword glanced off its neck armor, then it bolted toward the shadows.

The other mounted human struggled to control his horse. The beast shied away from the gnolls and the fire, and it started bucking. The spike-armored human clung to its neck until it stopped rearing. As the frightened animal turned, however, Grawltak saw another human clinging to the man's back.

"Down!" Kark cried out, diving toward his pack-master.

A crossbow twanged and the bolt streaked toward Grawltak's surprised face. Kark reached him first and the bolt struck the old gnoll in the side. He howled in pain as he thrashed on the ground. Grawltak stood in amazement for a moment, then he shook himself and snarled.

The half-orc was almost within reach and swinging his axe in mighty strokes. Gnolls fell or fled before him, and those who fired their bows either missed or saw them strike Krusk's heavy mail with little effect. Grawltak looked up into the half-orc's face and saw a ferocity he'd never seen before. He backed away cautiously, guarding himself with his axe.

Even as the half-orc charged, however, the shining knight

steered her mount to cut him off. Grawltak had a disturbing image of his mistress, then. He'd seen her ride that way, and he feared to face this soft-skin if she was anything like her.

"On, Krusk! Get on!" shouted the knight, her voice clear amidst the carnage. "Get up here now!"

Grawltak saw their plan: escape. Despite the ferocity of their attack, the soft-skins were still in a bad position. His gnolls were regrouping. They outnumbered the villagers and the fire was spreading quickly through the inn. If he could delay them, the battle could be a great triumph. With renewed nerve, he moved forward to attack the knight's horse.

The half-orc was having trouble mounting behind the knight. When he swung up onto the horse's back, he nearly dropped his axe, and something else did fall. Grawltak's eyes saw gold flash in the firelight and he stopped in shock. His mistress had explained to him in great detail exactly what he needed to capture from the half-orc. The packet on the ground before his feet bore the emblem she described.

The half-orc saw his prize lying in the dirt even as the knight spurred her horse. As Grawltak dodged the beast and lunged toward the packet, the half-orc actually tried to fall back out of the saddle. But the knight reached back and held him, screaming, "Krusk! Let it go! We must get out of here!"

The half-orc's wordless bellow ripped from his throat, but he could not escape the knight's steely grip.

Grawltak's guards jumped forward, swinging their axes at the knight and her steed. The gray horse leaped forward between them and rode away into the darkness. Grawltak snatched up the packet, and with one quick look to make sure his eyes had not deceived him, he stuffed it into his armor.

"Fall back!" he yelled. "Back!"

His voice was triumphant and his pack, though eager to slay the soft-skins in the courtyard and make the humans pay for spilling gnoll blood, obeyed their leader. Grawltak snarled at two of his uninjured scouts, and they picked up the wounded Kark and fled into the darkness with Grawltak close behind.

Three dead gnolls and several wounded humans lay in the village square. The inn's roof blazed, but the fire looked worse than it was. The villagers in the top floor kept the fire from spreading to the interior of the structure, tossing flaming bundles of thatch out the windows as quickly as they could fall into the rooms. Early clutched his side and hobbled over to Ian, who emerged from the upper floor, limping painfully.

"Did they get away?" Early asked.

Ian nodded.

"I heard that paladin yell something. Did it work?"

Ian shrugged and answered, "I don't know. The gnolls are gone. That much worked." He looked into the darkness, but even his half-elf eyes couldn't see their former companions. "I hope they got away safely."

Alhandra and Krusk, Regdar and Naull rode hard and fast along the road through the village. Windlass stepped nimbly over the ruts and wagon tracks but the brown mare Regdar had selected from the stable nearly fell twice. Finally, he had to call to the paladin to rein up. They dismounted, Regdar breathing heavily.

"It worked! I can't believe it worked!" he panted breathlessly.

Naull grinned and patted him hard on the back. "Why not? It was your plan. Krusk, you were amazing!"

The half-orc grinned, his fangs and yellowed teeth showing in the moonlight. It was the first time any of them had seen him really smile, and the sight made Naull laugh out loud.

"Here," she said, pulling out her plain, oilskin packet and handing it to him. "Careful. I stuffed everything in there, but I don't know if the clasp will hold."

"What did you put in the other packet?" Alhandra asked.

She'd missed much of the preparations, having been too busy climbing out the inn's side window and into the stable to see how the rest of Regdar's plan came together.

"Just what I had in my own," she said. "A few papers, nothing really—" She smacked her forehead. "Damn! I left the letter from the village with our contract in it!" She looked at Regdar in dismay. "We won't get paid!"

The fighter laughed. "Don't worry about it. I've got most of the orcs' loot in my pack. Early and Ian already got their shares," he said. "Besides, Eoghan'll need the gold to fix his roof."

They looked off toward the village. It was too dark to see, but they took that as a good sign.

"It looks like they put the fire out," Regdar said.

"I hope the gnolls leave them alone."

Alhandra said, "I think they will. When they realize they don't have the key, or the map, or any of the rest of it, they'll be too busy trailing us to go back to the village."

"Now there's a hopeful thought," Naull said dryly.

"It is," Krusk agreed, no humor in his voice at all. He shook his axe back toward the scene of the fight. "It is."

The other three exchanged looks, then Regdar sighed and said, "Well, we'd better get moving before they have a chance to look at their prize. Gnolls move pretty fast when they're mad, and these will be madder than a troll at a barbecue."

No one disagreed.

8

THE CANYON

"**Isn't this where** you just came from?" Naull asked as they entered the dark canyon.

She and Regdar still rode the horse they'd taken from the inn's stable, but Alhandra sat alone on Windlass. Krusk insisted he could keep up with them on foot, and it made sense to have him scout the path ahead. Naull couldn't see more than a dozen feet in front of her after an hour of riding, and it would only get worse.

She saw the barbarian's shaggy head move, but whether he was nodding or simply hopping over the stones, she couldn't tell. She sighed.

"Krusk, we can't see you," Alhandra reminded him.

They'd decided to do without torches. When the gnolls realized they'd been tricked and came after Krusk again, they would move more slowly if they were following a vague track than if they were following the distant light of burning torches. Regdar suggested they might dare lights once they reached the canyon's floor, but Naull wouldn't hold her breath.

"Yes," the half-orc grumbled.

Don't like to talk much, do you? Naull thought.

Still, she had questions that needed answers.

"So this is the way to the gate?" she asked.

A pause.

"Yes," the half-orc said again.

"Why didn't you just go there, then, instead of coming all the way north?"

The horse's hooves clacked and slid on the rock trail. Naull clutched Regdar's side to keep from spilling off their mount and onto the ground.

"Needed to find some help," Naull thought she heard, but Krusk's voice was faint.

"What was that?"

"He needed to find someone he could trust," Alhandra explained. "That's what he told me, back in the inn. He said he knows how to close the gate, but I don't think he can do it alone."

"He probably didn't want to lead the gnolls right to it, either, in the condition he was in," Regdar supplied.

That made sense. Naull started categorizing the rest of her questions, hoping Regdar or Alhandra would call a halt soon.

The party continued downward into the darkness. Eventually, Naull felt the ground under their horses' feet level off. The unfortunate animals still stumbled in the darkness, however, even Windlass, who seemed to have an uncanny ability to find the smoothest route.

"This is getting ridiculous, Regdar," Naull said. She could barely see their horse's head when she looked around the fighter's armored back. "Krusk may be able to see in the dark just fine, but the rest of us can't. Either light a torch or let's camp. I vote for the latter. I may have slept most of the day, but I'm exhausted. I'd like to prepare some spells tomorrow," she hinted strongly, "unless you think I can contribute to this little expedition with just my crossbow."

Regdar pulled up and Naull heard Alhandra do the same.

"That was a good shot back at the inn," Alhandra said from somewhere in the darkness. "It kept their leader off us until we could put on our little show."

Krusk grunted his agreement.

Despite herself, Naull felt her cheeks color at the praise.

"It was a lucky shot," she admitted. "I don't practice much with this thing, and Regdar can tell you some stories. . . ."

But the fighter didn't say anything. Instead, he dismounted and Naull scrambled down as well. She heard Alhandra dismount.

"Krusk," Regdar said, "find us some shelter. Some place we can defend, if there's anything suitable nearby. Naull, you've got the supplies?"

Naull nodded, hefting the bag Lexi had hastily put together for them before they fled the inn.

They set up a small, cold camp under an overhang on the east side of the canyon. Moon- and starlight glimmered down to reflect dimly from the rift's floor, fifty or sixty feet below. It revealed no detail at all, only a barely discernible glimmer. Other than Krusk, the adventurers were nearly blind.

"Campfire?" Naull asked.

"No," Regdar responded. "We don't need one, anyway."

Shivering in the shadows, Naull wanted to disagree, but Regdar was right. Their packs were loaded with dried meat, bread, and a few blankets. They wouldn't starve or freeze.

"Aren't deserts supposed to be hot?" she asked.

"Not at night," replied Regdar. "Krusk, I can take the first watch. I'll wake you in a few hours, and then Alhandra can take over from you."

"Don't I get a turn?" Naull asked, pretending hurt.

"So you can complain about how your sleep-deprived mind can't accept the magic patterns? No. We're not spending more than eight hours here. You sleep the whole time, starting now."

"Yes sir!"

She grinned and leaned over to pat Regdar playfully on the

cheek. He looked up at her and the warmth in his eyes made her blush.

Someday, she thought as she thanked Wee Jas for the darkness surrounding them, we might have to talk about this. But we're partners now, she concluded, lying back on her blanket.

Grawltak panted eagerly as he held the packet in front of him. They fled northward from the village and found a stand of trees to welcome them. They discarded the torches and lanterns as they ran—always into a convenient haystack or shack, of course. The soft-skins wouldn't forget this night in a hurry! He drew out his disk-shaped amulet and spoke the words that invoked its power.

A whine from Kark stopped him. They'd carried the wounded lieutenant away from the inn. Three younger whelps were lost in the battle and another failed to keep up on the road. If he managed somehow to catch up, then they'd consider bringing him along too. Otherwise, he was bait for the softskins. But Kark . . .

"Draw the bolt—carefully!" Grawltak instructed one of the gnoll pups.

He shoved the disk back inside his armor but held the packet eagerly.

Gnolls seldom knew much about healing, unless they became the chosen of Yeenoghu. Grawltak shuddered again at the thought of the shamans his mistress employed. She followed Hextor, he knew, but at least one of her pet clerics was a follower of the gnoll god.

Kark writhed in pain. Blood stained his mottled fur. He was unconscious and looked as if he would live, but his body wouldn't let him rest. Grawltak's dark eyes studied the older gnoll carefully, then he reached a decision.

"Give him this," Grawltak snapped.

He pulled a dark flask from his belt pouch. One of the younger gnolls opened it and sniffed it, but at a growl from the leader, he stooped and poured it between Kark's open jaws. At first, it seemed the older gnoll might choke on the elixir, but he coughed and stopped writhing. In moments his breathing returned to normal. His dark eyes opened.

"Leader . . ." he said, sounding almost confused.

As uncharacteristic as Kark's sacrifice back at the inn had been, it was obvious Grawltak's generosity surprised the old gnoll.

It surprises me as well, the gnoll leader thought angrily. That's the second time I've saved you from death, though at least this time it was in return for your favor.

He growled angrily, "I have to have someone to keep these pups in line! I have only ten left. Get them into order while I call the mistress or I'll have all your hides."

Kark stood stiffly and nodded. He turned his head, exposing his neck in supplication, but Grawltak turned away. The younger gnolls looked on in confusion, much as his pack had watched him years before when he'd first spared the old pack-master's life and made him his lieutenant. Grawltak knew he had Kark's loyalty, but the younger gnolls couldn't help but mistake his gesture— sharing precious healing magic with a mortally wounded under- ling—as a sign of weakness. Grawltak knew his alliance with Kark made him strong, stronger than other gnoll pack leaders, but he wasn't sure the rest would see it that way.

All thoughts of reestablishing pack dominance left Grawltak's mind as he took out the amulet again. He grinned, his tongue lolling to one side. His mistress would be very pleased with him. So the half-orc got away. So what? Even the mistress said the half- orc itself was of no matter, as long as what it carried was delivered to her. Grawltak would soon be rewarded, and his pack would see it.

Placing the amulet on a stone before him, he chanted the magic words. They weren't easy for the gnoll to speak clearly, as they were in a language even more foreign than the soft-skins' common speech. There was much hissing involved, and the sibilants made his jaws ache from forming the words.

Grawltak's perseverance paid off, however, and the amulet glowed. An image formed in its clear, flat face then tilted ninety degrees and rose up above the stone. A face—his mistress's unarmored face, glowing in various shades of red—hovered above the magic talisman.

"What is it?" the red face asked. The lips moved but the words made sounds at a different speed. Grawltak looked into the red, glowing eyes and reflexively turned his head.

"Mistress . . . it is Grawltak. I have succeeded."

The eyes narrowed, focusing on him.

"Bring light," she said. "I can barely see you, gnoll."

Grawltak cursed and shouted for a torch. Kark came forward and lit one. He held it off to one side, illuminating his leader's canine features.

"You have the half-orc? Finally?" The voice sounded impatient, but also pleased.

"No," Grawltak started, then hurried on as the image's eyes widened. "But we have this!"

He held up the oilskin packet. The flaming sigil gleamed in the torchlight.

"Open it!" demanded the red face of his mistress.

Hurrying to obey, Grawltak nearly dropped the packet and its contents to the ground. He fumbled it open and held it out to the face.

"Take everything out, fool! I cannot see!"

His claws moving as deftly as they could, Grawltak pulled papers and a few small coins out of the packet. Something was wrong . . . he stuck his snout into the packet, but saw nothing else. This couldn't be all his mistress desired.

"Open the papers! Show me!"

The sinking feeling in the pit of Grawltak's stomach started growing. His mistress hadn't said exactly what should be in the packet, but ... papers and a few meager coins? Very carefully, one by one, he opened the folded sheets and showed them to the face. He couldn't read them himself, but none looked much different from any other.

His mistress made him go through each and every page but Grawltak didn't need the darkening of the flame-face to tell him he'd somehow made a terrible error. Her voice grew more and more angry as he revealed each page more and more reluctantly.

When he picked up the small coins to show her, she shrieked at him, "Enough! You've been tricked, you idiot! Where is the half-orc?"

Grawltak didn't know what to say. The truth wouldn't do at all, he knew, but lying to the mistress ...

Kark broke in, "We are on his trail, Mistress. He is not far. He is wounded. I have his scent, but I am old and slow. Grawltak did not want to delay reporting to you. We will catch him soon."

Staring at Kark, the red face considered the older gnoll.

"Grawltak is a fool, then, old one," she said. "Capture him," she ordered, her eyes turning back to the pack-master. "Do not fail me this time, gnoll! I'll string your intestines along the ground and make your pack eat them for dinner." It was no idle threat, Grawltak knew. "And I'll make sure this old one is the first to dine."

Both gnolls nodded eagerly, their ears cocked forward.

"Where are you?" she asked.

Grawltak told her.

"Catch the half-orc. Do not kill him if you can avoid it, but I will join you soon, with the shamans. I should be with you in no more than a day."

The gnoll shuddered. It had taken them more than five days of hard traveling to reach their current position. If she could get to them in a day. . . .

"Mistress," Grawltak ventured carefully, "we do not know

where the half-orc might lead us. We should, as Kark says, catch him soon, but—"

"Do not worry, Grawltak," the red face smiled cruelly. "I can find you, wherever you are. Never forget that. Now, go!"

The face held their gaze for another second, then winked out. The amulet's glow faded.

Turning his head toward Kark, Grawltak started making the sign of thanks gnolls showed only to their leaders. Kark did not let him dip his head.

"You are my captain, pack-master. I live to serve."

With that, the older gnoll stood up and went to get the younger ones back in order.

Grawltak wondered at this one small spark of good fortune in a conflagration of disaster.

The night passed uneventfully in the canyon. When Krusk and Regdar woke, Alhandra was tending the horses and Naull sat reading her book. She looked at Krusk as the half-orc hopped up and stretched his muscle-bound, ugly limbs.

"I was cold all night," she said dryly.

"How long before we find the gate?" Regdar asked Alhandra as he strapped on pieces of his armor.

Alhandra shrugged, then looked over at Krusk. The half-orc drew out the packet, and with only a little hesitation, he tossed it to her. The paladin opened it and started looking through the papers.

"I can't read any of this," she said.

Regdar shook his head. He couldn't, either.

Naull stepped over to the pair. Krusk prowled around the campsite, as if looking for signs of danger.

"Doesn't Krusk know how far we have to go?" she asked.

"I suppose," the paladin answered. "Captain . . . Tahrain? He made Krusk repeat the directions to him when they fled the city. He has a wonderful memory, I guess."

They looked at the half-orc. He crouched in the sunlight near the middle of the canyon, looking up at the sky and blinking furiously.

"Let me see . . . Hey, it's in Draconic!" Naull said. "I suppose I shouldn't be surprised; the most common name of the City of Fire, Secrustia Nar, is draconic, too."

"You read Draconic, though, right?" Regdar asked hopefully.

"Of course. Most wizards write in draconic. It's a very old language, and hasn't changed much for centuries. Dragons aren't much for change," she added dryly.

"No, they just get bigger and nastier," Regdar added.

Naull flipped through the pages carefully. Someone had obviously copied them from the original, but the paper was still very old and stiff. She wondered, considering the legends of Secrustia Nar's age, how many times the descendents of the City of Fire's refugees had duplicated the contents of the packet, all the while preserving its secrets. She shook her head in amazement.

"It's tricky," she said at last. "It's in a sort of code. The first part is clear enough. There's a tunnel somewhere in this canyon, on the western side. The tunnel leads to another rift, or something like it. Beyond that, we're supposed to see signs that lead us toward the gate. That's where the code gets tricky."

"How?" Alhandra asked.

"Well, as near as I can tell, the code's arranged so that we'll find clues to solving it as we go, but it would be almost impossible to solve the next part of the code without actually following the path. Whoever made this didn't want you to be able to just decipher the code and jump to the end."

"Nasty," Regdar said.

"Why so much concealment?"

Naull answered, "Not everybody is as nice and trusting as we are." The paladin looked up sharply, but Naull smiled, taking a little of the sting out of her words. "Whoever did this wanted to make sure that if outsiders—people who didn't know the dangers of the trail—found it, they'd have to go through those dangers before reaching the gate. Since we don't have any of the original inhabitants of Secrustia Nar on hand, we're going to have to run the gauntlet."

"Oh, that's just fabulous," Regdar said. "Any idea what's in this gauntlet?"

"Well . . . not really," Naull replied. "I mean, I think it can't be all that bad. From the descriptions I can make out, it seems this was just a guarded trade passage, not a series of death traps. You wouldn't want to kill off visiting merchants just because they forgot the password."

That observation made both Alhandra and Regdar relax a little, but Naull secretly wasn't certain. Secrustia Nar's reputation was infamous in some texts she'd read, especially near the end of its days.

"Let's get started, then," Regdar said.

Travel through the canyon went slowly. Naull imagined Krusk moving through it alone, hopping, skipping, and sometimes running. She looked around Regdar's shoulders at the many caves and pits in the canyon walls. It seemed a terrific place to hide from enemies.

They ate quickly, giving Windlass and Stalker just enough time to rest. Regdar named his steed after the inn; Naull thought it an overly generous name for the nag. They walked the horses through narrow passes but rode them more often than not. Both Krusk and Regdar felt certain the gnolls would be right behind them.

"Surely they need to sleep, too," Naull said.

Krusk shrugged and said, "We were a day ahead of them in the desert, but they caught us."

"We have to keep pushing," Regdar concluded.

"Whoever this black knight is, she'll be pushing them," Alhandra said. She'd made sure Krusk related his description of the gnoll's human leader to the rest of the adventurers.

Naull shuddered. When Krusk spoke of the woman who led the attack on his companions, she heard the hate in his voice, and the fear.

Regdar reined Stalker to a halt.

Naull peered over his shoulder and asked, "Why are we stopping?"

"Krusk stopped."

Naull swung down off the brown horse and saw the barbarian looking up at the sky and at the west wall of the canyon. It looked like the rest of the rift; rough, rocky, and barren. There were a few holes in it, but nothing to set it apart from any other stretch of rock.

Krusk pointed.

Naull squinted up into the light. The sun had barely dipped below the west wall, where it glared unhelpfully right over the lip and into her face. Still she thought that perhaps she did see something.

"It looks like . . . is that a cave up there?"

Regdar and Alhandra dismounted and retreated from the west wall, shading their eyes. Drawing out the papers Krusk had allowed her to hold onto, Naull studied them. The first part of their trip was clear: Come to a certain point in the canyon and there would be a cave leading west. The papers said nothing about the cave being more than fifty feet up the canyon wall.

"This can't be it," she said.

Krusk didn't agree. He pointed toward the lip of the eastern wall. They all looked and saw a rock formation that resembled five teeth jutting up from the wall.

"No, no . . ." Naull disagreed. "There are supposed to be six of them, and they're supposed to be taller, and curved, almost like bolts of lightning or fire. Pillars of fire—there!" She pointed to one page that had a crude diagram.

Regdar looked over one of her shoulders and Alhandra the other. The fighter shrugged in half-agreement, but Alhandra pursed her lips and shook her head.

"Like you said, Naull, it's been what . . . centuries? Don't you think one of the 'pillars' might have fallen? And don't those look like the bases of pillars? The tips—the flames—probably wore away."

Nodding, Naull agreed, "Of course. I didn't think of that. What about the cave, though? This route was for trade caravans. Who's going to haul a wagon up the side of mountain?" she asked the others.

The paladin considered for a moment, then ventured cautiously, "Centuries . . . thousands of years, perhaps. Could this canyon have deepened, or widened since then? Maybe there was a river, or a stream, even—or there could even have been an earthquake."

Nodding agreement, Naull folded the papers and put them away.

"I suppose so," she said, "but who's going to climb up to make sure?"

The two armored figures looked at each other. Finally, Regdar shrugged and started taking off his armor. Alhandra stopped him and pointed.

Krusk, still wearing his chain shirt and with his axe slung over his back, was already climbing. Digging into the stone with his big hands and feet, he was nearly fifteen feet up the wall.

"Leave it to Krusk," Naull chuckled, shaking her head.

Alhandra smiled, too. Regdar, surprisingly, took out his bow. "Might as well cover him," the fighter said.

Moving to Windlass, Alhandra retrieved her own bow and strung it. Naull simply limbered up her fingers. If anything came out of the cave or down into the chasm, she didn't want to trust to her crossbow.

Krusk moved slowly up the cavern wall, occasionally stopping entirely. They watched at first eagerly, then warily as he made his way up the cliff face. Twenty feet . . . twenty-five . . . thirty-five.

If he slips now, Naull thought, we'll have to scrape him off the canyon floor with a stick.

Sure-handed and sure-footed, as well as amazingly strong, Krusk didn't slip. He reached the bottom lip of the cave mouth and pulled himself over. Moments later, he lowered a knotted rope almost to the canyon floor.

Regdar went up first, then Naull. Alhandra wrestled with her conscience, trying to decide what to do with the horses. Finally she led them around the next bend in the canyon and stripped them of their gear. What she couldn't carry, she hid in a shallow pit and covered with a rock. She emptied a waterskin onto a bowl-shaped stone hidden by shadow.

"I hope we won't be too long," the paladin said minutes later as Regdar helped her into the cave. They drew up the rope and Krusk tucked it back into his small pack. "Or that the gnolls don't find them."

Her voice sounded pained. Naull didn't say anything, but she saw Regdar reach up and pat Alhandra's shoulder. He looked over at the wizard.

"Well, what now?"

"According to the directions, we just head in. Krusk? Anything to add?"

The half-orc stopped for a moment, thinking, then he recited in a sing-song voice, "The passage leads down, down and around. Do not turn, do not vary. When you reach the floor, the key shows the way."

He blinked and looked at the others.

"All right, then. Naull, I guess we'd better use some light."

Krusk went into the cave first. He didn't need light to see, but the humans did. Alhandra brought out a small lantern from her gear and lit it. Naull debated lighting a torch as well, but she could always cast a light spell if they needed it. Walking behind Alhandra and in front of Regdar, she could see fine.

The passage descended, as the notes indicated it should. It was rough going at first, but as they proceeded farther into the darkness, the passage actually widened and the descent became smoother. Before they'd traveled a hundred yards, the passage was so wide they could easily walk three abreast.

Something about the darkness stopped them from spreading out. To Naull, the whole place felt eerie. Krusk moved at the edge of the lantern's light, but the three humans stayed close together. When they passed the first side passage—a narrow opening to the right—Naull wrinkled her nose at the foul smell.

"I hope there aren't orcs in here," she said, then clamped her mouth shut.

Her voice echoed in the darkness.

THE KEY

They passed turn after turn, passage after passage, always descending, always following the main tunnel. Naull lost track after they ignored more than three dozen side passages and her legs started growing weary. As they passed yet another shaft, this one to the left, she paused to examine the map and announced, "I think we're almost there."

Looking around, the party saw that a short distance ahead, the passage opened up on the left hand side. Instead of two walls and a ceiling, they saw a wall to the right but the ceiling and left wall were gone. Alhandra held up her lantern, but they couldn't see much in its dim light.

"Krusk?" Regdar asked. "Do you see anything?"

Peering into the darkness, the half-orc scanned the area. "Steps— thirty, maybe forty feet ahead. They wind down to the left then drop about forty feet," he said, leaning over the edge. "Flat area down there."

"That's all?"

Krusk nodded.

"All right; let's go. Be careful," Regdar added. "I don't want anyone falling off the edge."

They made their way down the passage and found the stairs quickly. Naull wondered how anyone managed to bring a wagon beyond this point but figured if there was a large, open area to the left they might have had some sort of unloading mechanism. It certainly wasn't important now. The stairs were smooth and slick with the cavern's dampness. The party moved cautiously, Krusk in front and Regdar at the rear.

About halfway down (as they figured the distance), Krusk stopped suddenly.

"Passages. All around the outside of the room," he said.

Regdar, who now followed the half-orc in the order, looked up at Naull.

"What do you think? Want me to light things up a little?" she said.

"Can you?" he asked carefully.

He remembered her light spells; they didn't provide much more illumination than a torch. She smiled back smugly.

I've been waiting for this, she thought, flexing her fingers in preparation.

She pulled out a small round stone she'd prepared and said a few words in Draconic. With a flash, the stone glowed brightly. In an instant, they were all blinking in daylight.

"Whoa!" Regdar shouted, surprised.

Naull grinned back. "New trick," she said, winking at him.

She tossed the glowing pebble in her hand and caught it.

"I'll say."

The cave looked like someone had torn the roof off and revealed the noonday sun.

They saw Krusk's passages almost immediately. The stairs curved down into the circular room, then ended a little more than twenty feet from where the party stood. A dozen passages, each sealed with a gate of some sort, ringed the outside wall. As they moved down into the open area, each in turn saw that the floor was covered with thin slime. They poked it warily, first with Naull's quarterstaff, then the tip of a dagger. Finally, Regdar pinched some of the residue between his mail-covered fingers and sniffed it.

"Normal," Regdar said, "but slippery, I imagine."

The party moved into the room and fanned out. A heavy-looking portcullis barred each of the passages. Naull walked up to one.

"Look at this!" she exclaimed.

The effect of the daylight spell stopped a few inches beyond the iron bars.

"Krusk," she called, "come over here a minute."

The half-orc sloshed through the mud, and at Naull's direction, he squinted through the iron bars. As he came away, he shook his head.

"Can't see anything," he grunted.

Naull held the daylight pebble up to the bars and hesitated. With a piece of string, she tied the pebble to the end of her quarterstaff and extended it between the bars of the portcullis. The light in the cavern went out suddenly. Someone—Naull thought it was Alhandra—gasped. She pulled the staff back and the light returned.

"What did you do?" Regdar snapped. He'd been startled, too.

Naull explained, "It must be a darkness spell—and a powerful one. It looks like there's one in each of these passages."

They looked around and saw that it was true.

"What do we do, then? Which way do we go?" Alhandra asked.

They stood in silence for a few moments, Naull idly tossing the pebble in her hand again. Then she remembered Krusk's recitation. She turned to the half-orc, who seemed to be testing the bars of one portcullis.

"Krusk! The key—you said the key would show us the way. Pull it out!"

Krusk paused only for a moment, then pulled the key out from beneath his chain shirt. The disk glowed again as he revealed it to them. In the effect of the daylight spell they could all see that the flat, flame-decorated key gleamed brighter than before.

But other than that, it did nothing.

"Try walking in front of the doors," Regdar suggested.

Krusk looked at Naull, then at Alhandra, and did as Regdar said. He held the key in his large, open hand and walked slowly around room. The rest of the party followed him, watching carefully for any sign from the disk or the passages.

Nothing happened.

"Well, that was no help," Naull grumbled. She picked up her right foot and looked in disgust at the slime. "Anybody see anything on any of the doors?"

Each portcullis looked identical and unmarked to her. Naull moved to the center of the room so the rest of the party could see every portcullis at once. She grew bored as they searched, however, and started flipping the stone in the air like a coin. The shadows in the room bounced up and down.

Finally, Regdar had enough. Breaking off his search at the sixth door, he strode to the center of the room and grabbed Naull's wrist in mid-toss.

"Stop that!" he said, frustration in his voice. "You're giving me a headache."

The pebble dropped past Naull's hand and plopped into the slime covering the floor.

"Oh, great," Naull said irritably as she crouched to retrieve it. "That's just great, Regdar."

She picked at the slime with her hands. Though the light centered on the pebble, it didn't make it any easier to find when it was covered in muck. She ended up having to sweep whole sections of the floor clean with her hand.

"Yuck!" she complained, flipping grayish slime off her fingertips. "I should make you do this, you know," she said to Regdar. "At least you have gloves!"

The fighter stared at the floor. Without looking away, he called out, "Krusk! Alhandra! Get over here!"

He crouched and started pushing away the muck with both

gauntleted hands. Slime splashed up into Naull's face and she recoiled, then slipped and fell onto the floor, the glowing pebble back in her hands.

"Hey!" she protested. Regdar shot her an apologetic look but kept on sweeping. "Hey!" Naull exclaimed again as she saw what he was doing. "Hey!" She got down on all fours and helped.

It took several minutes, but when it was over the four slime-soaked adventurers had cleared away a large section in the center of the circular room. The floor glistened damply, but with most of the slime gone, they could see what looked like a giant version of the key: A ball of flame emblazoned on the floor. The tail of the flame pointed quite distinctly at the third door from the stairs.

"Now that's more like it," Naull said, wiping her face with the back of her hand.

"But how do we open the door?" Alhandra asked.

As they looked from one to another, Naull had an idea.

"Krusk, stand in the center of the room," she said, "then pull out the key and orient it like the one on the floor."

The half-orc followed the first two directions, but balked at the third. Naull didn't understand what the problem was until Alhandra stepped up to him and moved the disk in his hand so that the tail pointed in exactly the same direction as the one on the floor.

"Right," Naull said, "now walk straight toward that door."

As Krusk stepped across the room, Naull thought she saw a faint light coming from beyond the portcullis. She and the rest of the party followed Krusk. As they neared the passage, they heard a faint creaking sound. Slowly, the portcullis rose. Beyond it, they saw a stone-lined passage, wide enough for all of them to walk abreast, lit by torches that had somehow sprung to life.

"I guess that's the way," Naull said.

They stepped inside.

A few miles away, up and to the east, other feet stepped inside a cave.

"Are you certain they came up here?" Grawltak growled fiercely.

The scout nodded. They had followed the soft-skins' trail from south of the village and only stopped once for a short rest. His gnolls were tired, but their noses still worked. They'd found the horses only a few hundred feet away. They slew the dark one, but the gray bolted farther into the canyon when they'd approached it.

The gnoll pack butchered the fallen horse and took as much meat as they could carry. They were messy and loud about it, but Grawltak let them enjoy themselves while he considered his next move. He pushed them hard, and would push them harder. If the soft-skins went underground, then they must be following the map his mistress said the half-orc possessed. He needed to keep pressing them, to catch them if possible. Horse blood would have to do for sleep and fresh-killed meat would have to do for rest.

Grawltak himself could not enjoy it. He needed to check in with his leader. Crouching down on all fours, he pulled out the disk and set it on a rock. He chanted until it glowed to life.

"Mistress . . ." he said.

The red face answered.

THE GATE

The hall continued straight as far as they could see. Every twenty feet a new pair of torch sconces were mounted on the wall, and each flared to life as the adventurers approached. Four pairs of torches lit when they stepped into the hall, and there seemed to be no end of them as they walked down the silent passage.

"Magic," Krusk said. He still held the key in his open hand and its flames flickered brightly.

"You think?" Naull observed dryly, but her nervous sarcasm was lost on the half-orc.

As the party continued on, they noticed the torches behind them didn't dim after they passed. The portcullis, it seemed, remained open as well.

"Do you think we should go back and close it?" Naull asked Regdar. The opening seemed small and far away, but it was clear in the light.

He shook his head. "No. If we need to get out of here in a hurry, I don't want to try to figure out how to open it from this side. Besides, do you know how to shut it?"

Naull shook her head.

"Then let's keep moving."

The passage continued for several hundred feet. It stayed straight and level, and the width never varied. Reddish flagstones covered the floor, large enough that only two and a half were needed from wall to wall. The walls appeared to be made of burnished sandstone, but they were smooth to the touch and not porous at all. The ceiling, which was rounded and stood at its highest point nearly thirty feet from the floor, was darkly colored but had shades of red as well. They saw no dust or dirt anywhere.

"This is just creepy," Naull said at last. Regdar nodded. "I mean, we've been in some pretty nasty goblin tunnels, and that passage down here was nowhere I'd like to stay for any length of time, but this is so, so regular. I've never seen anything like it."

"Dwarf-make," Krusk said, but he didn't sound certain.

"I don't know, Krusk," Regdar answered. "I mean, dwarves are pretty good with stone and all, but even their work fades after centuries. I don't want you to bite my head off—" the fighter turned to Naull—"but do you want to check for magic?"

The wizard shook her head. "I don't," she said. "I mean, I'm sure the torches are magical, but they could really just be a triggered version of a continual flame spell. That's no big deal. Whatever magic keeps these passages intact and completely clean after all these years . . ." She shook her head. "I've heard stories of powerful magic blowing the backs of wizards' heads off when they try detecting it. I'll be perfectly happy if nothing like that ever happens to me. Let's just say I cast my spell and determined that, yes, this whole place is magic, all right?"

Regdar smiled at Naull's speech, and she grinned back, feeling a little better. Another pair of torches flared to life.

Alhandra, who was walking a little ahead of the party pointed with her sword and called out softly, "Did you say 'clean,' Naull?"

The others hurried up. About eighty feet ahead, just at the farthest edge of the torchlight, the party saw that the passage opened up. It looked like it might be a room, but they couldn't see beyond the reach of the torches. Just where the hall widened lay what looked for all the world like bundles of ripped or discarded cloth. Clothing, perhaps, and other bits of gear.

Regdar drew his sword from its back sheath. Krusk, like Alhandra, already had his weapon in his hands.

"A trap?" Naull asked.

"Maybe," the fighter answered. "Could be what's left of the last people who came down here."

Naull looked over at Krusk, who tucked the key into his chain shirt.

"But nobody's been down here for centuries," she said. "They couldn't get here without the key."

"Maybe there are other keys," Regdar answered uncertainly.

"Whatever it is, we aren't going to find out much from here," the wizard stated finally. She started walking forward.

With a sharp exclamation of alarm, Regdar jumped forward.

"No—wait here," he said. "I'll check it out."

"I've seen how you find traps, Regdar," she said, mimicking him striding forward and looking oblivious. She jerked up short, flailing her arms and overbalancing as if her foot was caught in a noose. "Look! A trap!"

"Very funny, but that bit of cloth isn't going to protect you if something shoots out of the wall," he said, jabbing Naull high in her sternum.

"Well . . . let Krusk come with me. He's good at spotting things, and I can try to find any magic."

"What about getting your head blown off by arcane forces?"

"I'll chance it," she said. She crooked a finger at the barbarian, who shuffled forward. "C'mon. Let's see what there is to see."

Despite her jaunty attitude, Naull felt her stomach churning as she and Krusk moved toward the open area. Regdar and Alhandra followed them until the torches in the room—four of them, spaced evenly around the walls—flared to life. The room looked to be about thirty feet in diameter, and a door stood at the far end.

On the floor they saw several piles of ragged clothes, bits of old adventuring gear, and even a few glittering gems. Naull easily resisted the urge to jump forward and examine them. It wasn't the time to be greedy. In fact, their presence made Regdar's guess about the trap seem even more likely.

Although, she wondered, if people died here, where are the bodies?

"Anything about a door in that memory of yours, Krusk?" she asked in a low voice.

The barbarian paused again, and his lips started to move. He had to run through the litany front to back.

". . . a door at the edge of magic," he began aloud finally, "the key will come to life. Open the door to see the light and reveal the gate."

Quickly, Naull shuffled through the papers in the packet. She looked into the room—they still stood twenty or so feet from the entrance—and at the door. She saw an image of flame graven into the stone door. It looked similar to the image of the key, but not exactly the same. However, to the right of the door, at about waist height, she saw what looked very much like a keyhole.

"Yes!" the wizard cried out. "This is it!"

She stuffed the papers into her pouch and stepped forward into the room. As she stepped past the first pile of debris, the rags on the floor sprang to life. Krusk cried out in warning, but he was too late.

The gnolls wrinkled their noses as they picked their way down the passage. As trackers, they welcomed the advantage a strong scent afforded, but these smells from below ground were unfamiliar and unsettling to the scouts.

"Keep moving!" Grawltack ordered, cuffing the nearest scout. "Follow the trail."

The younger gnolls jogged ahead of him, but Kark held back. The two older gnolls followed, keeping out of earshot of the rest.

"What did she say, Grawltak?" Kark asked in a low voice.

The pack-master cursed and clutched the magic amulet, as if by doing so he could keep his mistress from hearing.

"She was not pleased. I do not think she expected the half-orc to lead them to the caves so quickly."

"How could she think otherwise?" Kark snuffled disrespectfully. "She didn't know where the passage was. She didn't even tell us we were looking for a passage!"

Grawltak thought of reprimanding the old gnoll for his candid comment, but sighed tiredly. "She has not told us other things, either. She insists that we follow and that she will find us before we must enter . . ." he hesitated.

The mistress had been very clear in her instructions. "Do not tell your followers this, Grawltak," she had said. "Follow the half-orc to a city—a magic city, with great treasure in it. Stop the half-orc from entering, or you enter yourself and slay him and all with him."

She said other things, too, things he needed to consider carefully before going much farther, but he continued, "We must enter a passage. The passage leads to a gate, which leads to a city." He shot a look of warning at Kark, and the older gnoll understood and nodded. "I cannot tell you more, but if we do not catch the half-orc and his friends, we'll have to go into the city and . . . and that's something I do not wish to do."

He growled, deep in his throat. Gnolls seldom admitted to fear, and never to their subordinates, but Grawltak was tired and Kark was his friend.

The old gnoll nodded and asked, "And she will find us?"

"She will, curse—curse the half-orc," he amended. He nearly tore the amulet off his chest. "I'm not sure I want a reward anymore, Kark. The mistress drives us, and I do not think we will gain a reward anyway. I would rather go back to the north and raid."

Kark chuckled and let out a soft howl of laughter. Despite himself, Grawltak found himself chuckling, too.

"Would that we could!" Kark said. "But we must hunt our quarry and kill it. Only when the half-orc's blood stains our fangs and we tear out the throats of his friends will we be free again!" He clapped his leader on the back. "Come, my captain, let us join the hunt before the young ones run into trouble."

Grawltak grinned and the two set off down the passage.

A strip of dirty cloth leaped up at Naull from the floor. She started in surprise and moved her fingers, but the band wrapped around her hands and arms tightly. She tried to cry out, but another strip whipped at her face and drew blood. When she opened her mouth, rough leather gagged her. Eyes widening in panic, she tried to pull away.

Krusk hacked at the cloth, yelling his war cry. He narrowly missed hitting Naull as she felt herself jerked back and forth by the animated cloth. As the tatters and bands of leather and fabric wrapped around her, she felt herself spun this way and that.

From the corner of one eye she saw the other bits of ripped clothing fly up off the floor. They formed roughly humanoid shapes. Bits of gems and metal peeked out from behind the tatters, and the shapes jerked as if manipulated by a puppeteer's strings.

One of the shapes leaped, or flew, or in some other way moved toward Krusk. He still tried to find a way to strike the fabric grappling Naull and the shape caught him from behind. The half-orc cried out as strips of cloth and leather bound his mighty legs. Dropping his axe, the half-orc wrestled with the tattered form.

Then something struck Naull—from inside. Something that felt like a ragged but powerful consciousness tried to envelope her mind even as it covered her body. She tried to scream again, forgetting the leather bonds around her mouth, then she fell back on her training.

Concentrate . . . concentrate, she thought.

In an instant, she felt the consciousness repelled. It could not control her as long as she maintained her focus.

So the fabric started squeezing her.

Alhandra and Regdar rushed forward as they saw the cloth snake out and grab Naull. They reached the room as it completely covered her and as Krusk dropped his weapon. Regdar shifted his bastard sword to his left hand and drew a knife. He tried cutting at Naull's bonds but succeeded at slicing both the fabric and the wizard underneath. With a cry of dismay he hardened himself and hacked again. The fabric shuddered and Naull's blood flowed, but the creature was shifting to avoid the blade and that meant it was releasing the wizard. Naull gasped as air came back into her body.

Alhandra paused at Krusk's side to help him, but a third tattered shape leaped toward Regdar. Alhandra rushed between the fighter and the magical horror and swung her sword down. It cut through the humanoid shape easily, shattering one of the gemstones in the process. The floating rags uttered no cry, but did recoiled as if in pain. Stepping forward, Alhandra raised her arm to strike again.

Before she could slash through the jumping fabric, something smashed against the paladin's unprotected back. If it hadn't been for her fine steel armor, the blow from Krusk's axe would have severed her spine. As it was, Alhandra stumbled forward in agony, her own blade slicing wide. The tatter-creature retreated before her, though, and she turned to see Krusk raise his axe again.

It was Krusk, and it wasn't. He was wrapped up the same as Naull, but his eyes were open and staring blankly, not even focused on Alhandra. His axe came down and she dodged aside easily.

"Krusk!" she cried out. "Fight it off!"

But the barbarian didn't seem to hear. He swung his axe again, this time less clumsily. The leather and fabric wrappings gave him the appearance of an unraveling mummy, but whatever force was at work had him completely under its control.

With Regdar's help, Naull finally jumped clear of the grasping creature. The moment she was free, two bolts of force jetted from her palms and struck the rags in what should have been their chest. Fabric shuddered, then fluttered harmlessly to the ground.

Alhandra continued blocking and evading Krusk's powerful blows, but another of the rag monsters was moving up on her other side, trying to get behind her. Either it would get her or Krusk's axe would, that seemed certain.

Picking up his sword again, Regdar jumped behind the half-orc. Turning the blade to the flat, he didn't hesitate. In a mighty, two-handed blow he brought it down on the half-orc's skull.

Krusk turned toward him and swung his axe.

Regdar cursed and deflected the blow. Alhandra, seeing Regdar in danger, moved forward and swung her own blade, one-handed but flat side out, at the back of Krusk's head. The second blow was too much even for the half-orc's thick skull, and the fabric-covered barbarian went down. The cloth and leather strips unwrapped from his still form and jigged above him, but two more magic missiles struck them and the rags disintegrated.

Glittering sparks erupted from the sole remaining creature, blinding the adventurers. When their eyes cleared moments later, it was gone.

"Krusk—is he all right?" Naull asked as she bent to the barbarian's still form. Alhandra was there as well, while Regdar stood over them, watching for any attack. Nothing came, however, and Alhandra drew off her gauntlets.

"He's only unconscious," she assured Naull. "He'll be all right." Still, she placed her hands on the half-orc's face and they glowed faintly.

"What were those things?" Alhandra asked.

"I'm not sure," Naull said. "I've heard of creatures that live at the borders between worlds, but . . ." She slapped her forehead lightly. "I should have known there'd be something like this. The City of Fire is on another plane. There's bound to be strange things in between."

Krusk blinked his mismatched eyes and groaned, forestalling any more of Naull's self-recrimination.

The wizard smiled, then winced. "I think it broke one of my ribs," she gasped painfully.

"Here, let me see," Alhandra said.

She helped the wizard down onto her back as Krusk shook himself off and stood guard with Regdar. A warm feeling moved through Naull's body and she felt the slicing pain in her side ease. It was still there, but reduced to a dull ache. She noticed that the cuts on her arms were closed up as well.

"Thanks," she said, allowing Alhandra to pull her up. The paladin winced in pain, though. "Oh, I'm sorry," Naull said contritely. She remembered the massive blow Krusk had struck her in the back. "Get that breastplate off. Let me look at it."

Alhandra shook her head and rubbed her back. "No . . . I'll be all right. Let's look at the door."

Frowning, Naull let the matter drop. She wasn't a healer, anyway, but she wanted to do something. Still, her spells killed two of them. How could she tell the rest of the group she had nearly exhausted her store of spells again? She was still thinking of what to say when Krusk drew out the key.

The disk blazed to light immediately, as brightly as they'd seen it yet. A sigil inscribed just above the lock answered by turning fiery red.

"Well, go ahead," Naull said.

Krusk stuck the key in the lock. It went in about three-quarters of the way, so he could still hold it in his big fingers.

The outline of the emblem on the door glowed brightly and a long, straight crack appeared in the opening. The door split in two and swung open.

THE CITY OF FIRE

Bright light spilled into the torchlit hallway. Each adventurer blinked and Krusk raised one thick forearm to shield his mismatched eyes. The light was brighter than Naull's new spell, brighter even than true daylight.

"Stairs," Regdar said as his eyes acclimated.

The others looked and saw a flight of sandstone-colored steps leading up into the bright light.

"Do you see anything else?" Naull asked. She still shielded her eyes with her hands. Peering into the light was painful.

The fighter shook his head and moved forward.

"No," Alhandra said, "it's my turn."

The paladin, her armor shining brightly in the clear light and her sword held before her, advanced toward the light.

The others followed at a short distance, Regdar second, Naull third, and Krusk bringing up the rear. Of all the adventurers, the half-orc seemed to have the most problem with the bright light and he didn't lower his arm away from his eyes.

Naull found as soon as she stepped onto the stairs, however, that the light became more bearable. She still couldn't see the top of the flight, but as she slowly ascended, the light bothered her less and less. By the time she'd climbed a dozen steps, she could see normally. She looked back and Krusk was no longer shielding his eyes. His heavy brows still squinted against the dazzle, but he peered around more or less normally.

"I . . . I think I see something," Alhandra said, pausing on the stairs. The others stopped behind her, but the paladin started moving almost immediately. "It's . . . it's . . ."

Standing on the top step, Alhandra lowered her sword and looked around in amazement. The others followed her example. Naull gasped audibly, and Krusk growled.

"It's the sky," Regdar said.

"It's *a* sky," amended Naull.

Beyond the stairs the adventurers saw an open expanse above them. It was red, however, not blue, and the few wispy clouds swirling quickly through the air high above them seemed almost bright pink in color.

Naull shook herself out of her wonderment and said, "That passage . . ." The wizard hesitated. How to say it without panicking anyone? "That passage must have been the link between our world and the plane, the pocket dimension, that Secrustia Nar resides in. We're somewhere between our world and the Elemental Plane of Fire."

Turning in place, Regdar gaped at the wizard. The others looked at her.

"We walked to another plane?" Regdar asked.

Naull shrugged, palms upward, in answer.

"Oh," he continued, "I thought there'd be some big, swirling gate filled with fiery energy or something, not just a hallway."

Krusk thumped Regdar on the shoulder, who looked at the barbarian, and asked, "What?"

Pointing one finger over the fighter's armored shoulder, Krusk nodded. Regdar turned.

"Oh," the fighter said simply.

The sky still swirled red above them, giving off light with no sun, but all around the land looked much more familiar—flat, unremarkable desert. That is, except where Krusk pointed. Perhaps a quarter mile distant—it was very hard to judge distances—stood what looked like a huge arch. It was sandstone in color, like the stairs, but an immense emerald-colored stone flashed in the keystone at the top.

Within the arch, reddish-orange flames rippled.

"Well, isn't that nice?" Naull commented dryly.

Regdar frowned, but then grinned at her.

"Let's go," the fighter said with mock exasperation. "I want to get this over with."

The others followed.

"I thought it was supposed to be harder than this," Regdar whispered to Naull.

Alhandra took point again, and Krusk walked with her over the hot sand. All four sweated furiously.

"You complaining?" she asked, but privately agreed. She took out the papers that came with the key and shuffled through them as they walked. "The key," she said. "It must be because we have the key." She looked down at a picture on one of the sheets. "Either that, or . . ."

"Or what?"

"A lot of this stuff," she said, shaking the papers and wiping sweat off her forehead with her sleeve, "has to do with the city itself. I thought it told of the dangers and tricks for getting in, but . . ."

"But it talks about the dangers *in* the city."

Naull wasn't certain, so she shrugged almost apologetically. "It really is a weird code."

Regdar stopped, and Naull halted alongside him. "Naull," he said quietly, facing her. "No one expects you to know everything or to be able to figure it all out. We're getting swept along here, and you're figuring things out as you go." He reached out to her and she took his gauntlet in her hand. "You're doing great."

Nodding, Naull smiled up at her partner.

Yes, she thought, we're definitely going to have to have a talk when this is over.

"Thanks," she said.

The two turned and continued walking, and the party reached the gate sooner than they expected. It loomed large in front of them, but not as large as they'd supposed from the end of the stairs. It stood perhaps forty feet high and was easily thirty feet across—nearly a semicircle, jutting up out of the sand.

"Heironeous protect us!" Alhandra exclaimed, holding up her shield. "It feels like an oven!"

It did. The flames in the gate weren't just for show. The adventurers felt as if they stood in front of a well-stoked forge, if that forge was the size of a large city gate.

But there was no city beyond the gate. They looked on either side, and after a few moments of arguing Krusk actually walked all the way around the arch.

"Here!" Krusk exclaimed.

Just above head-height on the left side of the arch they saw an emblem that looked exactly like the key. Krusk pulled out the golden disk and raised it, but Alhandra shouted for him to stop. On the other side of the arch was a second emblem, identical to the first. After a few minutes examination, they found two more, each on an opposite side.

Pressed deep into the stone of the arch, each emblem looked identical to every other. Naull confirmed from the notes that the right thing to do was place the key into one of these emblems. That would open the arch and let them into the city ... but which one should they choose? Krusk had no more information from Captain Tahrain. He stood before the gate, sweating and staring at the flames.

"I don't know how much more of this I can take, Naull," Regdar complained. "Could we at least move away from this thing while you figure it out?" He'd stripped off his helmet and poured water down into his armor. Alhandra did the same, but they didn't dare use any more of the precious liquid that way. "Should we go back to the stairs?"

The wizard sat before the fiery gate, laying some of the papers out before her. She found a diagram of the arch and it had small symbols on it she guessed were the key sigils. Naull shook her head once, sweat from her head spattering the ground.

"No . . . no," she said, "there has to be a clue."

"Well, what do you know so far?" Alhandra asked.

She stood by the right side of the arch, running her hand over the stone. Her face glistened in the light. Naull resisted the urge to scream at her.

It's the heat, she thought. Regdar's right—we should move away from the arch, but didn't the paladin ever . . . ?

"Wait . . ." Naull said. "I think I've got it."

She jumped up, clutching one of the pages in both hands. Moving quickly to Alhandra's side, she pointed to the sigil there.

"Look! Here, the tail of the flame goes up and to the right."

She jogged over to the other side of the arch, the others following tiredly, and Naull indicated the emblem there.

"Here," she said, "it points to the left. On the other side—" she moved around the arch—"it's reversed, and upside down. It's the same sigil but it's oriented differently, relative to where you are near the arch."

Shaking his head, Regdar asked, "What does that mean?"

"Don't you see? The key can be placed in any of the emblems, but it has a different function depending on which you use."

"All right, I guess that makes sense," the fighter mused, rubbing his goatee thoughtfully, "but why four emblems? What does each one do?"

Naull grinned as she suddenly realized the answer.

"That's what hung me up for so long," she said. "Two sigils would make sense—one to open the gate and one to close it— but four? That's what had me puzzled."

She started chuckling, shaking her head. When she looked up, even the paladin stared at her with a twinge of impatience.

"Oh, sorry," Naull laughed again. "Look up at the sky; what do you see?"

They all looked up and Krusk, surprisingly, was the first to answer, "Fire."

Alhandra and Regdar gaped, but Naull nodded sagely and said, "Right. Fire. That isn't a red sky up there—that's actual flame."

It took a moment for the import of that statement to sink in.

"No wonder it's so hot," Regdar added lamely.

"It was Krusk who made me think of it, actually," Naull said. Stooping, she picked up a handful of sand—or tried to; she dropped it almost immediately. "It's really hot. But now feel the air." She breathed in, deeply. The others followed suit. "I know it's hard to tell, but the air isn't hot. It's certainly warm, but most of that's emanation from the sand. I bet the air's no hotter than it was back in Durandell."

The others agreed, but they still didn't understand.

Naull continued, "Before we opened the door back there, this area was part of the Elemental Plane of Fire. In fact, I'm betting it still is—but it's been changed, magically, to someplace we can inhabit. That's why there are four symbols on the arch."

"All right," Regdar said, following Naull to the left side of the arch. "I understand. So a few hours ago, this area was completely covered in flame."

"I guess."

"And it'll be covered in flame again?" Alhandra ventured.

Naull shrugged and said, "I guess so—probably when somebody closes that door."

They all looked nervously back at the hole in the sand.

"So how do we open this gate?" asked Regdar.

"Krusk, will you loan me the key for a second?" Naull asked.

She stepped up to the left side of the arch and the half-orc handed her the golden disk. It flashed with its own light when she held it up to the archway, but didn't touch the emblem.

"See, I figure that two of these symbols are for us—people from our world—to use. The other two are for denizens of the Elemental Plane of Fire to use. Secrustia Nar doesn't lie on our plane, or the Plane of Fire, but between, remember? You'd need a key to get in or out, from either place."

"So all you have to do is try each of the symbols, and the gate will open," Alhandra said.

"Well . . . yes," Naull allowed.

Regdar caught the uncertainty in her voice and asked, "What's the catch?"

The wizard sighed, "The catch is, if we put the key in the wrong symbol and it thinks we're coming from the Elemental Plane of Fire, I think the magic will . . . adjust to make us more comfortable."

It took a moment, but even Krusk got the idea.

"Krispy Krusk," he said.

The joke was so unexpected, Regdar barked with laughter and slapped the barbarian on the back. "Well, we can't have that. So which is the right one, Naull?"

She looked up at the symbol before them and said, "It's really the right *pair* we have to worry about, Regdar. If we put the key in the wrong keyhole, so to speak, as long as it's one of the right pair, we're all right. It'd be like trying to lock a door that's already locked—no harm done."

"So we have a fifty-fifty chance," Alhandra observed helpfully.

"Somewhat better than that, I hope," Naull answered. "No, I'm pretty sure we want to use the symbols with the tail going up and away. Think back to the symbol on the floor and the others we've seen. Even all the inscriptions on these papers always present the image of the key in pretty much the same way. The ball is at the bottom, the tail at the top. The sigils on the other side of the archway are the first time we've seen them upside-down."

The party began to breathe a little easier. It made sense.

"And, as far as which is the right one to open the door," she said, standing on her toes and placing the key just above the symbol but not pressing it home, "Draconic is a very left-first sort of language. It reads left-to-right, important words are arranged in the beginning of sentences, and so on. I think this—" she looked at the others, who nodded— "is the correct one to choose."

She pressed the symbol home and flames belched from either side of the archway as a deep rumbling shook the sand under their feet. The party scrambled away from the archway moments before fire erupted outward. The shaking of the ground threw them off their feet and Naull scrambled to a sitting position.

"Of course, I could be wrong . . ." she shouted over the tumult.

Down in the circular room the gnolls heard the rumbling and felt the ground shake. A few yelped in panic and ran for the stairs.

"Stay!" Grawltak snarled.

He tore his bow off his back and strung it in an instant. Kark followed his lead. The younger gnolls saw their leader's eyes flash in the dark and they stepped back down, away from the stairs. He growled at them and they whimpered, baring their necks.

"Something's happening," Kark supplied unhelpfully. Grawltak barked in annoyance.

"Go—find out what," he said. "Take these cowards with you. I must summon my mistress."

She'd told him to make contact when they reached the city gate or had the half-orc in tow. They had neither, but something told Grawltak it would be best not to delay any longer. Pulling out the amulet, he sat down on the damp floor. He did not wait for the rest of his pack to lope down the passage before he began his chanting.

The red face appeared and Grawltak relayed the recent events. The rumbling, at least, had stopped, but that didn't seem to please his mistress. She swore effusively when he told her of their progress.

"They can't be more than half an hour in front of us, Mistress," he whined. "I've sent my pack to capture them, but I knew you'd want to hear this news."

"Curse you!" the red face said. "Very well . . . you were right, Grawltak," she allowed grudgingly. "You've failed to capture the half-orc or stop them from entering the city, but you did guess right in this. I am coming. I will be there momentarily."

Reflexively, the gnoll blinked and looked over his shoulder, up the stairs to the passage beyond, as if he expected to see his mistress descending even as they spoke. She caught his movement through the amulet and laughed cruelly.

"No, gnoll. I would have preferred not to do this, but—"

The face turned away and Grawltak saw her lips move, though no sound came to him. Then the red face composed itself and closed its eyes. The amulet started to shine brightly. As the light intensified, Grawltak scrambled up on all fours, then backed away.

There was a blinding flash and the sound of metal shattering. A piece of shrapnel hit Grawltak's bare wrist and he yelped. When he looked up from the scratch he gaped. His mistress, clad in her dark armor and bearing her sword and shield stood before him. Her sword glowed with a dark light, somehow illuminating the room without really dispelling the darkness. He fell to his knees.

"Get up, fool." Her booted foot crunched on what remained of the hopelessly shattered amulet. Whatever magic it once held was completely gone. Grawltak didn't feel relieved, however—he'd traded the amulet for the real thing. "Lead me to them," she said.

Without a word, the gnoll moved off toward the lighted passage. The blackguard strode behind him, her dark armor flashing in the torchlight.

The adventurers rolled in the sand as the quaking slowly subsided. Naull spit dirt out of her mouth and pushed Krusk's big arm off her waist. The half-orc sat up, trying to rub his eyes clean with sand-encrusted paws. Naull made him stop and used a little of their precious water to clean his eyes. Behind her, Alhandra gasped.

The gate was clear, Naull could see, but from where she sat, almost even with the left side of the arch, she could see nothing remarkable on either side. Alhandra stood directly in front of the archway, staring through it. Scrambling onto her feet, Naull looked through the gate and added her gasp to the paladin's.

"The City of Fire . . ." she said.

Through the archway, the adventurers saw a city. It filled the gate and obviously continued above and beside it—but the desert around the arch remained unchanged. A road on the other side of the arch led straight into the city.

"The portal is open," Naull declared as they stared in wonder.

Krusk recovered first. Taking the key off the arch, he stepped through the gate and started walking down the road at a brisk pace. There was no strange transition between worlds—he stepped through the arch as if it was just another passageway. Naull cried out and hurried after him. The paladin and the fighter brought up the rear. Krusk kept going as if he'd walked that path every day of his life.

The rest of the adventurers hurried to follow, but they couldn't help but look at the wonders before and around them. The City of Fire was aptly named. It was filled with colors—most of the buildings were white or sand-colored, and there were blue and green gemstones decorating some of the windows—but by far, red and orange dominated the view. Windows were made of tinted, orange glass and what had to be magical flames served as pennants on the tallest spires. The towers were tall and straight but almost always topped with onion-shaped roofs. Those few that weren't seemed entirely flat, as if made for someone or something to land upon them.

"It's cooler here," Alhandra observed.

Indeed, there seemed to be a soft breeze wafting down the

avenue toward them. They all inhaled deeply from the crisp air, then continued on.

For several minutes, the adventurers were content to follow Krusk's lead. They watched the flames of the city dance and marveled at the gemstone decorations. Eventually Regdar's sense of apprehension grew and he stopped the half-orc.

"Where are you going, Krusk?" he asked, seizing the half-orc's gray, muscled bicep.

The barbarian turned, fierce determination on his face. He growled and looked down at Regdar's hand, but the fighter didn't release him.

"Must close the gate. Permanently," he said finally.

Regdar nodded. That's what the half-orc had promised his dead captain, and that's what they'd come to do.

"But how?" Regdar asked. "Do you have any idea what you're doing?"

The half-orc's determination slipped for a moment and he looked less sure. Naull hurried up to them.

"We have to find the palace," she said, pushing a page from the packet under their noses. "It says the rulers of the city could control everything from there. If there's a way to close the gate permanently, it'll be there."

Alhandra added her voice to the debate. "But how can we find the palace? Is there a map?" She looked around. Many of the buildings might be considered a palace back in her homeland.

Shaking her head, Naull said, "No, but I doubt it'll be hard. These papers refer to an 'Ivory Tower' and an 'Opal Throne'."

Krusk made a noise and started in amazement. "Opal . . . Throne?" he asked.

"Yes. It says right here: 'And the great caliph sat with flaming crown/The tower of Ivory/His Opal Throne.' I think it's a poem, but it really doesn't translate," she added. "It talks about how the caliph could control the city from the throne, so I'm guessing the throne is some sort of magical device."

The half-orc's normally gray face seemed ashen. "My captain," he breathed. "Captain Tahrain's title—he was 'Protector of the Opal Throne'."

"I'm guessing Kalpesh didn't have an actual Opal Throne, then?" Naull prompted.

The half-orc shrugged. "Many jewels—some opals. Never thought about it."

"Why would you?" Regdar asked, putting an arm on the barbarian's slumping shoulders. "And what would it matter anyway? At least it explains something about how this packet was protected. Your captain, Tahrain, must've been the last in a long line of protectors. It was his job to make sure nobody got the key and the power of the Opal Throne."

Krusk looked up, his eyes dark and his face grim.

"Not the last," the half-orc said.

He clutched the key to his chest, and an awkward silence followed.

"All right, then," Naull said at last. "Let's find this ivory tower. It shouldn't be too hard. I guess Krusk had the right idea. Keep walking along the main road and we should come to it, or see it."

"Maybe we could ask for directions?" Alhandra joked.

Regdar and Naull grinned.

"There you go. If only everyone hadn't fled the city thousands of years ago...." the wizard said, snapping her fingers and smirking.

Laughing with false bravado, they followed Krusk along the road.

Flames flickered off in one of the side-streets and a shadow moved. It leaped from one small building to the side of a tower. Soon, another joined it. And another. As the adventurers walked down the road, shadows and flickering lights grew unnoticed on either side of them.

Kark led the gnoll pack through the torchlit hall and down into the room. They found the tattered remains of the creatures that attacked the party, but did not know what to make of them. A few of the younger gnolls squabbled over the gemstones they found until Kark growled fiercely and they fell back into line. One of the scouts lifted a piece of leather and sniffed.

"Blood," he said.

"Whose?"

The young gnoll sniffed again, then tasted the dark red liquid. "Human," he answered.

"Half-orc," another said from off to one side.

There were several specks of blood in the room, and many of the pieces of fabric looked torn or ripped as if by sword or dagger. A few of the gnolls yipped with pleasure.

Kark snarled, "You don't see any bodies, do you? Save your laughter for when we have our quarry by the throat. Now—up the stairs!"

The younger gnolls whined and shied. Kark commanded them only by Grawltak's loaned authority, and even though it was less than an hour since their leader had sent them out, Kark could sense resistance. Gnoll packs followed one pack-master, and that leader ruled by strength and strength alone. The young gnolls saw an old curiosity before them—a live ex-pack-master. It was something they'd never seen before, nor likely would again.

Seizing the nearest gnoll, Kark drew the surprised scout in close, his claws digging into the creature's shoulder. The younger gnoll yelped in surprise and pain as Kark bit the back of his neck and tore a hunk of flesh and fur away. Before the scout could use his youthful strength to break free, Kark pushed him away and leaped toward the rest. Blood dripped from his lower jaw.

"Grawltak says we follow, so we follow!" he barked. "Until our pack-master rejoins us, I lead!"

He glared at the gnolls and knew they'd been cowed, at least for a time. The injured scout gripped his wound in pain, but dipped his head as meekly as the others.

"Now—up the stairs!"

The gnoll pack came out of the stairs and into the bright light far more reluctantly than the adventurers had. Kark had them in charge, but the light was so bright it burned their eyes. They shuffled and whined, snuffling at the ground for some scent, but the shifting sand made it difficult to find any trail.

Kark shielded his eyes and looked around. He could not see the archway—gnoll vision wasn't good in bright light—but fortune aided him. A few dozen steps away from the stairway he saw a rag half-buried in the sand. He loped over to it, the rest of the pack following. It was a discarded end of a bandage, with some blood still fresh on it. It gave him a direction and he led his pack that way. They moved slowly across the sand, not daring to miss another sign.

"Regdar," Naull whispered. Krusk and Alhandra were out in front again. "I've got to ask you a question."

"What?" Regdar replied. He was looking around again, this time not in wonder, but worry.

"Have you seen—"

"Things moving in the shadows?" the fighter interrupted.

Naull nearly jumped. "What? No . . . I was going to point out all the gemstones. This place is rich!" But now she looked around apprehensively. "What do you see?"

"At first I thought it was just the flames—shadows flickering and all that, but I'm sure—there!"

Regdar pointed and Naull whirled. She thought she saw something move between one of the buildings.

"Alhandra! Krusk! We've got trouble," Regdar said. He drew his big sword from its back-sheath. "What've you got, Naull?"

"Not much," the wizard said grimly, mentally adding 'like always.' "Maybe a surprise or two."

The adventurers stood in a square, back to the middle, as more shapes moved around them. Some were shadowy, but others looked as if they were made of fire. Knowing that the adventurers clearly saw them, they seemed less interested in stealth. At least a score of the figures closed in or darted among the buildings and spires.

"Get ready," Regdar said, without much hope.

Most of the figures were small, but he'd gotten a good look at a few of them. Several were made of fire, others of smoke. The few that were humanoid were naked and wreathed in fire or smoke and had a distinctly devilish appearance. Slowly they closed in.

"Now!" the fighter shouted, stepping forward to swing at the nearest creature.

"Stop!"

The gnolls sniffed at the archway suspiciously. They saw the city and the street beyond, but none of the pack crossed the threshold. All of them panted in the heat, desperately uncomfortable.

Kark, too, sniffed at the arch again and stared at the gem gleaming on the top. The adventurers went through it, he had no doubt.

Grawltak's orders were to follow their quarry and capture them if possible. The mistress, however, hadn't wanted Kark or the others to know about the city, and he didn't think she'd be pleased if they entered without their leader. He did not know what to do, and he'd been thinking about it since reaching the arch nearly a half-hour before.

Where is Grawltak? he thought.

In that thought, Kark decided—I follow my pack-master, not a soft-skin.

He feared the mistress, but he was loyal to the gnoll who spared and healed him. He knew no other gnoll, except perhaps Grawltak himself, would make the same choice, but he knew what he had to do.

"Come!" he snarled.

The other gnolls looked at him in surprise and concern, but a quick bark had them stepping through the archway and prowling the city's streets.

Grawltak remained below. His mistress set off down the passage on his heels but she stopped several times, as if unsure of something. When they reached the room at the end of the hallway she did not say a word, but he watched as she drew a wand from her robe and gestured around the area. She frowned and stood still for several minutes.

The gnoll pack-master didn't dare disturb his mistress—not for ten minutes, then not for twenty. When thirty passed he made a soft barking sound, as if clearing his throat.

The black knight looked up suddenly, her dark eyes glaring as her hair tossed behind her. He could not think of her as a softskin when she looked at him like that. He feared his fangs would break if he ever even tried biting her.

"What is it?" she snapped.

"Mistress, they went up," he said, pointing at the stairs.

"I know! I know, but if they entered the city . . ." She shook her head, then said in a low voice, "No, they do not know its secrets. They cannot use its power, not yet. It is useless to delay."

But she continued to hesitate. Grawltak shifted uneasily, his claws scraping on the floor. Was his mistress afraid? He shook his head and growled at the thought. What she feared did not bear thinking about.

"All right!" she said suddenly, but not to him. "I will go."

Without a glance in his direction, the black knight stepped onto the stairs and Grawltak hurried after her.

The power of command resonated in that voice. Regdar halted in his tracks with Naull's hand pausing halfway to a spell pouch. Krusk and Alhandra looked up and saw someone standing on one of the lower building's flat roofs.

"Stop," the voice rumbled again.

The dancing, fiery figures on either side of the road continued flickering but they stayed as still as flames ever could, in a ring around the adventurers.

The voice came from a short, stocky figure. He looked like a well-muscled dwarf but his skin shone as if it were made of brass. Instead of hair and a beard, orange flame wreathed his face and swirled up from his head. He wore a kilt made of some coppery metal and a surcoat woven of thin wire and studded with many gemstones.

"Disperse." Smoke rose from the creature's bright eyes as he spoke again.

Almost as one, the small figures surrounding the adventurers jumped and danced back between the side buildings. Within seconds, no sign of their presence remained.

The fiery dwarf looked around, apparently satisfied, then he strode down a set of steps leading from the flat roof to an alley adjoining the road. He walked right up to the party and Alhandra, who stood nearest his side of the street. The emblems on her shield and breastplate caught his attention and he nodded.

"Hail, servant of Heironeous," he said, holding one hand up in a gesture of peace. His mouth barely moved when he spoke, but his baritone voice rumbled from deep in his throat.

Alhandra recovered quickly. Sheathing her sword smoothly, she mirrored the dwarf's gesture.

"Hail, and well met. I am Alhandra, paladin of Heironeous."

The dwarf nodded, his flaming hair flickering as he did so. His face looked grim, but he bore no weapon, only a thick rod tucked into his belt.

"Welcome to the City of Fire," he said. "I am Gurn Klaggesar, warden of the city."

"W-Warden?" Naull stammered. "But we thought the city deserted."

The dwarf stared at her, his eyes smoldering—and not metaphorically. It was disconcerting, Naull thought, to look into eyes that burned like coals.

She shifted in the brief silence, then stammered, "Oh, I-I'm Naull, a wizard of . . . well, a wizard."

"No one dwells here, Naull the Wizard," the dwarf answered, "save I and my servants. We watch over Secrustia Nar and protect it from outsiders."

Naull fidgeted again, and Regdar said, "We're glad to hear it. We have the same mission."

A fiery eyebrow cocked and the dwarf looked at the fighter in what appeared to be mild disbelief, mixed with a small measure of amusement.

"I'm Regdar, and this is Krusk. He comes from the city of Kalpesh. He bears a key."

Krusk, suddenly aware of the dwarf's attentive gaze, fumbled in his pouch and drew out the key. He gasped and nearly dropped it. He'd grown accustomed to its magic nature—flames seemed to dance along its edge whenever he held it out—but now it appeared to be a ball of living flame, flickering and burning in his palm. Still, it gave off no heat and the half-orc's thick skin was unscorched.

"I am aware of the key," the dwarf said evenly. "I wondered when it would return." He sounded almost disgruntled, as if talking to children who'd 'borrowed' something that did not belong to them.

Krusk bristled and closed his fist over the ball of fire. "I come from Kalpesh!" he declared loudly. "My master was Captain of the Royal Guard and Protector of the Opal Throne. He died protecting the key and he passed it on to me. I will close the gate." His chin jutted out and his eyes bulged, daring the dwarf to respond.

Naull gaped and readied herself. It was one of the longest, most eloquent speeches the half-orc had given since she'd met him, and it seemed particularly ill-timed. Whatever this dwarf was, they stood on his home ground. She forced herself to look away from the defiant half-orc and over toward Gurn Klaggesar.

Surprisingly, the dwarf stepped up and bowed low, his flaming mane flickering. When he finished and spoke again, his voice changed. It was still strong and full of authority, but there was some respect there, too.

"Forgive me," he said at last. "I have not had visitors for many years. My manners are suspect. Please, let me welcome you, Protector, and your companions. Come, and I will show you the Opal Throne you have traveled so far to see."

The dwarf paused to see Krusk and the others nod, then he set off down the road with the travelers spread out on either side of him. He began talking, telling the story of Secrustia Nar.

Most of Gurn Klaggesar's tale echoed what Naull had already told the group of the legends, but some of it amazed her as well. It was a long tale and most of it made little sense. Still, Gurn had a way of telling a story that made the details interesting, even though none of the adventurers knew the people and places he spoke about. Eventually the dwarf got to the point of his tale, however, and each listened intently as he told of the creation of the city.

"Your world still breeds mighty wizards?" Gurn asked after some time. He looked at Naull pointedly and she nodded. "Then you know how they can be. Always delving, always probing for knowledge . . . and always looking for new ways to express their powers.

"Well," the dwarf continued, "a millennia—or was it two?—ago, powerful wizards from your world on the Material Plane made alliances with some of the beings dwelling on the Elemental Plane of Fire. They bargained with the efreet—" the dwarf spat that word out like a curse—"the azer—" Gurn indicated himself— "and others. With the aid of their magic, my people built this city between the two worlds and made it accessible to both. Beings of both planes can exist here; the magic sustains all."

"I told you it was dwarves," Krusk interrupted.

"Yes, you're very smart, Krusk," Naull said impatiently. She was eager to hear what the dwarf—the azer—imparted to them. The wizard studied the planes from books and scrolls; here, she had an actual denizen of one of the Inner Planes! "Please, Gurn, continue."

"There is not much more to tell," the azer said. "At first, the peoples of both planes dwelt together in peace. Good, evil, fire, and flesh. Magic and truce kept all in check and there was much commerce." The azer's eyes flickered at that word and Naull wondered how similar these fiery dwarves were to those she knew from home. "But conflicts arose. I know not what pressures built on the Material-worlders," he said, though his voice sounded a little harsh, "but some of the most evil creatures of Fire, the *zegguthi'ter ata garra*—"

The flames around the azer's head, which had been mostly bright orange, turned dark red and his bronze face darkened visibly.

"Excuse me," he apologized, and his face lightened, "the efreet—" again Gurn spat the word— "used their powers to corrupt and influence others. War began on both planes, and the city became a conduit for conflict and chaos."

"So you closed the gate," Naull concluded.

The azer nodded solemnly.

"But why didn't you shut it permanently?" Regdar asked. "I mean, if it's such a danger . . ."

"The city itself is no danger. It is a conduit through which many can draw power. Beings from either plane can come here, or be forced here, by any who know how to do so. The controller can then send these creatures out to perform services," he said. His voice was grim. "That is what started the war in the first place. Creatures of fire have some power on the Material Plane, no?" The others nodded their agreement. "And wizards still use them to fight their battles? Imagine if they did not have to use their own magic to summon and control creatures of fire. How dangerous would someone with that sort of power be?"

Naull thought of the little she'd seen done with summoning spells and the flaming sky outside. She shuddered.

"As to your question," the azer continued, not waiting for an answer, "the gates could not be permanently closed without also collecting all the keys. I could not leave the city to retrieve them. I sent out searchers for the keys long ago, but . . ." Gurn shrugged. "Most of the keys were stolen and scattered over many planes. I and my allies retrieved all of them but this one. The key taken to Kalpesh was not stolen," he said, looking at Krusk again, "but taken there for safekeeping while we searched for the others. As long as one remained, however, the gate could still be reopened."

Krusk started to open his hand again, perhaps to offer the burning key to the azer, but the dwarf turned away and gestured up and away from them. The adventurers' eyes followed his hands.

"Here. We have arrived. Behold the Ivory Tower! Inside you will see something no one from your plane of existence has seen for centuries. *Othakil eb Anar*—the Opal Throne."

The party stared in wonder.

The building that led to the tower was a wide, sandy structure set back from the road they walked along. It stood two tall stories high and marble statues with blazing, ruby eyes graced its court-yard. The party's eyes climbed the steps to the grand entrance but continued upward to where a white tower, so slender it had to have been built by magic, grew up out of the mansion. It continued up into the sky to end at a minaret made entirely of flickering flame.

"Well," Naull said at last.

The party entered the palace, walking underneath a marble dragon's legs. Winding stairs led up on either side of the building and small figures flitted over them, through the air and along the banisters. Many leaped to the side of the azer and he bent to listen to their wispy, crackling voices.

"My servants," he said. "Mephits and fire spirits and creatures of smoke. They spied you entering the city and told me. They will serve you as long as you are here."

The party nodded and Naull asked, "Do you have somewhere we can clean up?" She didn't know how long they intended to be there, but the wizard felt very tired and very dirty.

It's all this white, she thought.

"Of course," Gurn began, but then a small figure, a naked woman of perfect proportions but with fire instead of hair, hopped up to him and tugged on his kilt. He bent and his eyes widened as she spoke. "No!" he said. He turned to the party, his coal-black eyes now red with flame. "Others have entered the gate! How— there is no other key!" He glared accusingly at Krusk. "You left the gate open!" he said angrily.

The sudden change in their host's manner startled Naull, but the half-orc bristled and met the azer's stare. Before he could respond or Gurn could say anything further, Alhandra interrupted.

"The gnolls," she said. "We didn't realize they were so close behind us. We raced them here."

Quickly, the party told Gurn an abbreviated version of Krusk's story, and of their own flight into the caverns and down through the passage. He did not react to the burning of Kalpesh, but his eyes smoldered when he heard of the blackguard. He called the fiery woman to his side again and spoke to her in a strange language. She responded in kind, shaking her head.

"My servants have not seen—" he paused, as if considering,

then continued, "—a human woman in black armor," Gurn said with obvious relief, "but there are many of these gnolls. They must not reach the palace."

"Can't your servant . . . ?" Naull gestured, but her voice trailed off. At least one of the azer's mephits looked to be made of lava and others seemed to consist entirely of fire and smoke. "Can't they stop the gnolls?"

Gurn shook his head. "No—the compact with the Inner Planes is inviolate. They cannot harm anyone of the Material Plane while they are here. I will not be the one to shatter a treaty that has stood for millennia. You are of their home world; it is up to you to repel them."

"Oh, terrific," Naull said tiredly.

The Last Battle

The azer and his servants led Regdar and the others quickly into what looked like a small guardroom.

"I, too, cannot help you fight. If the blackguard reaches the citadel . . . perhaps," Gurn said, shuffling through a small chest. "But I can give you the means to battle. You, wizard."

He gestured to Naull. She stepped up beside him and he handed her a small black wand. As she touched it, one end glowed red.

"Point the bright end at the enemy and say *'secrus'*," the azer explained.

Naull nodded, recognizing the draconic word for "fire." She had little doubt of the wand's function.

"Krusk," he continued as he drew a quiver of arrows out of a small, nearly empty weapons locker, "use these arrows. I think you'll find them effective."

He gestured to Regdar and pulled out the last weapon, a bastard sword covered in runes that were burned into the blade with acid and treated with burgundy dye. He grinned, the first time they'd seen him truly smile. His teeth were white, but smoke wisped out between them.

"I think you'll like this," the azer said to Regdar.

"Paladin of Heironeous," he continued, "I have nothing for you. When the dwellers between worlds abandoned the city, they took or destroyed nearly all the weapons and magic within. Even if I could find something you might use, you would rather trust your sword and shield, marked as they are by your god?"

Alhandra shifted and said, "Don't misunderstand, sir. I will turn any weapon, unless it was created in evil, to the service of Heironeous, but I trust my sword and shield well enough. You are more than generous."

Gurn nodded sternly, but appeared pleased by the paladin's words.

"Perhaps I have something for you after all," he said.

From his own surcoat the azer drew a gem hanging from a silver thread. The paladin bent at the waist and Gurn laid the necklace over her head solemnly. It hung down over the emblem of Heironeous and both glowed briefly, the emblem gold and the gem red.

"Accept the blessing of Moradin," he said.

She nodded, apparently surprised to hear the dwarf god invoked by a creature of the Inner Planes.

"I will go up into the tower," Gurn concluded. "When you have defeated the gnolls, or destroyed them, return. We must work quickly. I can begin the process of closing the gate, but you must bring the key and its protector." The azer pointed at Krusk deliberately. "I cannot close the gate without you, and it."

Krusk nodded.

"C'mon, folks," Regdar said, hefting his new sword. "Time we got rid of these dogs."

"What are they?" asked one of the scouts.

The gnolls strung their bows and nocked arrows but Kark

ordered them not to fire. The creatures dancing in the shadows on either side of the road approached no nearer than the walkways and did not threaten them yet.

"They aren't human," the gnoll said.

Kark snarled, "I can smell that." His ears lay flat against his head. "They aren't attacking, anyway. Keep moving. Find the soft-skins."

The gnolls moved along the road, spread out and snuffling. Three scouts up front, three behind, and Kark and three others in the middle. They would find their quarry, and they would kill them. Kark believed the soft-skins couldn't run much farther.

He was right.

One of the forward gnolls, the one on the left, stopped suddenly. He yipped softly, just loud enough to draw the attention of the others. As Kark looked up, he saw a jet of flame stream down from one of the nearby buildings and strike the scout high in the chest. Fire burst around the gnoll, and he went down hard, his bow clattering on the stonework. The fire sizzled briefly, charring the dead scout's fur and sending up a horrid stench. Even before his nose caught the filthy odor, Kark barked an alarm.

Too late for the middle scout—an arrow made entirely of flame blasted the next gnoll as he turned. The young gnoll howled in fright and fear, beating at his fur before the fire could catch. Another arrow, this one made of wood and feather and tipped with steel, struck him high in the chest. He spun away from the impact, trying to flee, but stumbled and fell dead.

Kark barked orders, trying to rally his remaining troops, but they were frightened. The scouts were experienced ambushers, but they'd never before been caught in one themselves. Kark realized immediately that their prey had doubled back on them, letting the gnolls follow the trail right into a trap. The old gnoll knew from experience how effective that trap could be.

Krusk and Regdar kept firing arrows at the frontmost gnolls. They saw the old one move and heard it shout, but many of the others stood in shock and surprise or simply crouched, unsure what to do or even where to look. They were easy targets for the two archers.

Following behind one of the smoke mephits (Gurn would not allow them to fight, but he instructed them to guide those who could), Naull found herself winding through a narrow alley up to a small building on the right side of the road.

"*Secrus*," she breathed again, and a tiny red bead shot from the bright end of the wand.

Streaking toward the rearmost gnolls, it exploded against the skull of the centermost creature. The fireball's roaring eruption hurled two of the creatures to the ground encased in flame. They thrashed and shrieked for brief moments before falling still. Naull could see their blackened, shriveled forms inside the subsiding fires. The older gnoll, however, avoided the brunt of the blast by diving to the side. He rose from the ground quickly, looking distinctly shaken and with burning embers of his former troops still smoking in his fur.

From the other side of the road, Alhandra leaped out with her sword unsheathed, crying, "Heironeous! Heironeous!"

The gnolls that were still on their feet had their bows in their hands and were hungry for any target. Two arrows whipped past the paladin before her bright blade hewed through the hard wood and sliced into the creature's hyena-shaped skull. The sword wedged tightly in the bone, but Alhandra used her strength and momentum to wrench it free. She heard the beast's neck snap from the twisting motion, and Alhandra knew that whatever life may have remained in the creature was snuffed out then. Nimbly she leaped over the humanoid's corpse and rushed toward the next in line.

Kark's command disintegrated. With his flesh singed and his followers dying, the old gnoll wondered at the suddenness of the onslaught.

What happened? he thought wildly.

The silver knight he recognized from the inn's yard, but he couldn't even see the others. Flames and arrows and bright swords—Kark knew the fight was over when the knight stepped toward the last of his scouts. The last! From ten to two in mere seconds! Among the pack, there was no tradition of honor demanding that a commander die with his troops. Kark fled.

Seeing the last gnoll sprinting over the stone road, Regdar tried to line up a shot but couldn't. The angle was too sharp. He cried out to Krusk, but the barbarian already had his axe in his hand and was running to help Alhandra.

The paladin didn't need the aid. The only remaining gnoll discarded its bow and attacked with its axe. Alhandra caught the overhead blow on her shield and drove her sword through the creature's belly. Blood soaked into the heavy fur and ran down the blade to drip from the hilt. The gnoll slumped to the ground with its jaws still snapping. Desperately it clawed at the armor-sheathed leg that Alhandra placed on its chest, to no effect. Moments later, after a quick swipe of the paladin's sword, it too lay still. By the time Regdar came down from his perch, the fleeing gnoll was long gone.

"I could get used to this," Naull said, stepping out of the building. She looked appreciatively at the red-tipped wand, then tucked it in her belt.

"One escaped," Regdar said with a frown.

"Yeah, but this time we don't have to chase him," the wizard concluded. She cursed her choice of words immediately, knowing that Regdar didn't need a reminder of the disaster in the orc lair.

Regdar gazed down the street for a moment. Naull stepped up and put a hand on his arm. She looked at him with worry in her eyes but he met her glance and smiled wearily.

"It's all right," he said. "I think we're almost done here."

Then we can talk, Naull thought. She patted his arm and looked around. With a cry of revulsion she jerked her hand away from Regdar and clapped at Krusk.

The barbarian was moving through the fallen gnolls with a knife in one hand and several pointed, fur-covered ears in the other.

"That is just disgusting, Krusk!" the wizard cried.

The half-orc looked first from the wizard, then to Regdar, and finally to Alhandra. The look on the paladin's face made Krusk's dark cheeks flush slightly and he let the ears fall back to the ground.

"That's better," Naull said. "Now, if they have any treasure...." she added wispily.

"No," Regdar said, "let's get back to the tower. Let's get this finished."

Kark reached the archway, panting from the pain of his wound and the heat of the gate. When he looked up from the hard ground he grunted in surprise. Grawltak stepped through. The older gnoll started to cry out for his leader but the bark died in his throat. An instant after Grawltak appeared the black knight followed. He hadn't really believed she could reach them so quickly. Kark's heart sank and he let his head fall. He heard Grawltak curse and his leader moved to him quickly.

"Kark! What happened?"

There was nothing to do but tell the story of his failure. Without looking at the black knight directly, Kark gasped and panted through the tale of the ambush. He made no excuses, and when he looked up he was surprised to see pity in his leader's eyes.

Pity vanished in the raw gasp of a sword leaving its sheath.

Both gnolls looked over at the black knight. The point of her sword hovered only inches from their eyes. The blade trembled slightly and they knew it was rage, not fear or weakness, making the sword tip dance.

"Mistress! No!" Grawltak cried.

Kark continued panting but didn't move.

"He failed. Would you rather I held you responsible?" the blackguard said. Her voice was smooth, almost conversational, and she moved closer.

The blade slid directly under at Kark's chin, but the woman's pale face and bright eyes turned toward the gnoll leader. Her black hair seemed to shine in the flickering light of the gate.

Grawltak looked at his old lieutenant. There was only resignation in Kark's eyes. He expected to be killed, here and now.

"Yes," Grawltak said. "It was my decision to put him in charge. It was my responsibility."

Kark opened his mouth to gasp in surprise, but that made his lower jaw hit the blade and he closed it again. The woman, however, simply cocked an eyebrow and smiled in amusement.

"Gnolls aren't supposed to be loyal to each other, Grawltak," she purred. The gnoll leader started at the sound of his name on his mistress's lips, but he recovered his composure quickly. "Perhaps you are a little like dogs, after all." A moment later she put up her sword. "Very well. Don't think I've spared either of your hides yet. If we don't gain control of this city. . . ." she said ominously, gazing around for the first time. It was a long gaze, and it gave the two gnolls a few moments to recover and for Kark to gulp down a little water.

It was unnerving, though, the way the blackguard stood there, her eyes gleaming and her lips curled into the human version of a smile, Grawltak thought.

When Kark recovered, Grawltak said, "Let's go, then."

Waking out of her reverie, the black knight looked down at the two gnolls and nodded. Kark turned to retrace his steps back into the city but a word from the blackguard halted him.

"No, there is no time," the woman said as she pulled off her pack and drew a large bedroll from a pouch that was much too small to hold any such thing.

Magic, Grawltak supposed. He'd had just about enough of magic, he decided, but the gnoll leader remained silent as his mistress cut the straps and shook out the blanket. No, not a blanket, he saw clearly, but a carpet. Kark snarled with fear as Grawltak tried to understand what his mistress was doing.

Stepping onto the carpet the knight simply said, "Come here. Hurry."

She sat cross-legged in the center and Kark hesitantly crawled over the fabric to plop down beside her, his ears pressed flat against his head. He dug his claws into the carpet and looked at Grawltak. The older gnoll whimpered slightly with apprehension.

Suddenly, Grawltak knew how his mistress planned on traveling. His stomach tightened but he stepped onto the carpet. Almost immediately, he felt it ripple and move beneath him. Without a doubt, Grawltak knew he would not enjoy the next stage of the trip at all.

"We did it!" Regdar shouted as they entered the base of the palace.

No one greeted them. A few of the smoke creatures hovered near the stairs, but when the outsiders approached, the creatures fled up onto the next floor. The party looked around.

"He said he'd be up in the tower at the Opal Throne," Naull offered.

"Which way is that?"

As if to answer Alhandra's question, one of the mephits slid down the right banister and bounced to a stop at Regdar's feet. The fighter bent toward it but the creature hopped back up onto the rail and slid up and away. The heroes understood, following hurriedly up the staircase. The mephit led them to a wall at the top where a door slid open, revealing a circular closet with no ceiling.

"What? In here?" Regdar asked.

Krusk craned his neck and looked up inside the doorway. The smooth, rounded walls extended to the end of the half-orc's sight.

The creature bounced again and Naull took it as a nod. Cautiously, the wizard stepped into the room and took a deep breath. Alhandra followed with Regdar beside her. Krusk didn't venture inside until the mephit's bobbing became jumps of agitation, and the half-orc finally shuffled in.

The door slid shut and the adventurers heard a rush of steam below their feet. Warm air blew up all around them and a distinctly hot fog enveloped their feet, ankles, and lower legs. Naull bent to see if there was a vent near the floor, but Krusk bellowed in surprise and lurched against her. Naull tried to push the half-orc away and feel around for the vent but when her hands reached the "floor" she realized it wasn't there.

"We're flying!" Naull shouted.

Regdar put a hand out to touch one of the white walls but Alhandra seized his wrist in alarm. When the party peered closely at the sides of the chamber they realized the uniform walls were moving by very quickly. And, while it felt like they still stood on firm ground, Naull explained to the party that they were actually standing on a cushion of smoke and air.

"How did they do this?" Alhandra asked. After the initial shock, the paladin seemed to enjoy the trip.

"I wish I knew," Naull answered with obvious envy.

She looked over at Regdar, who returned her glance. He, too, looked like the ride met with his approval. Krusk, however, stood close to the center of the room clutching his elbows and holding his eyes tightly shut. Alhandra broke out of her wonder at the magic to step up to the half-orc's side. She touched his bicep and his eyes popped open. Naull and Regdar watched as the paladin whispered something to Krusk and the barbarian seemed to relax slightly. He took two deep breaths and nodded.

"Look!" Naull said, pointing up.

From the ground none of them had been able to see any end to the white walls, but now a dark ceiling approached rapidly. Krusk bellowed but even as he scrambled to put his hands over his head, their upward movement slowed, then stopped. They came to rest at least twenty feet below the ceiling and a moment later, one of the white walls opened, letting some of the mist spill through. With Krusk leading, the four adventurers exited the tower, followed by the mephit.

"Solid ground," Krusk grumbled, stomping.

Naull and Regdar grinned at each other but looked up as Alhandra stepped beside them and stopped suddenly, her hand smacking into Naull's back.

Slightly annoyed, the wizard twisted toward the paladin but then her eyes caught sight of the world around her and she forgot the bruise on her back.

From street level, the minaret of the White Tower looked like a bright flame at the end of a tall, white staff. Even though Naull knew they stood in a planar area between the Elemental Plane of Fire and the Material Plane, she'd assumed the flaming tower was no more than an illusion, a bit of glamour to give the White Tower more visual impact. Palaces were supposed to be brilliant and even Naull had been to enough cities to see that rulers spared no expense to decorate their homes and impress visitors.

They've outdone themselves here, Naull thought.

She ignored the white stone of the wall behind them. The rest of the room was fascinating. The floor looked rough and red below her feet, like molten lava, but it felt smooth and firm and the wizard sensed no heat rising through her boots. Flowing out from the center, the lava floor stopped at the walls, if she could call them walls, and Naull followed slowly, her left hand outstretched. The walls were transparent and appeared to be—no, they were, the wizard decided with conviction—made wholly out of live flame. Red, orange, gold, and yellow tongues danced up from the edge of the tower's floor, but did not mar her view of the city below. It was, indeed, as if she was in the midst of a torch's fiery end, but the air felt cool and comfortable.

"Welcome to the Opal Throne," a voice behind her said.

It was Gurn, and as Naull slowly turned she saw her companions doing the same, marveling at the tower's structure and the view beyond.

If the tower itself was impressive, however, the Opal Throne was magnificent. There was no doubt the chair the azer stood by was the Opal Throne—it could be nothing else—and Naull felt herself gasp as she looked at it for the first time.

Carved from a single giant opal, the throne's smooth, round features made it appear comfortable and welcoming. The light of the flaming walls gave the whiteness an almost living hue, and Naull felt that if she sat on the throne she would feel warm, secure, and comfortable. Indeed, the arms of the chair appeared to open for her as she watched. Naull stepped forward.

"A gift from the Elemental Plane of Earth," the azer said, stepping in front of it.

Naull shook her head and blinked. *Was I actually thinking of sitting in the throne?* she wondered. The thought was ludicrous. Looking around, however, she saw Alhandra and Regdar both looking as if they were coming out of a similar reverie. Krusk, however, had a hard look in his eyes and he scowled at the white seat.

Regdar spoke first. "We did it," he said simply. "We killed all the gnolls but one. They hadn't gone more than a quarter of a mile from the gate when we ambushed them. One escaped, but he was wounded."

The azer nodded and asked, "The blackguard?"

"There was no sign of her," Alhandra answered, but she sounded uneasy.

Gurn frowned and tugged at his fiery beard. He turned toward the Opal Throne.

"She is coming," Krusk announced.

The azer turned back and looked at the half-orc, and the rest of the party turned to Krusk as well.

"How do you know?" Naull asked.

"The gnoll's leader. The one who bears the axe and sword. He was not there."

"No," Regdar said, "the leader was the old one. He was just on the edge of the fireball. He barely escaped."

Naull thought back to the inn yard and with a sinking feeling she remembered.

"Krusk's right. When we dropped the packet, I remember an old gnoll and a gnoll with two weapons. The younger one was shouting orders, I think. It was all so fast . . ." She held up a hand as Regdar started to speak. Turning to Krusk, Naull asked, "But why does that mean the blackguard is coming?"

"She follows my trail. In the desert, the gnolls struck first, but the black knight came after. Her hounds follow our scent and she comes behind."

"Maybe she got left behind, in the caves?" Alhandra offered.

The half-orc remained firm. "The gnoll with two weapons was the pack leader. He would not let another lead his pack without a terrible reason. Someone he fears commanded him to stay behind. She comes with him now."

"Why would she want him to—" Regdar argued, but Alhandra interrupted.

"Regdar, if Krusk's right, we don't have any time to waste. Even if he isn't, we have little to lose by being thorough."

The fighter thought for a moment, then nodded and said, "All right, so what do we do?"

Regdar looked over at Naull, but the wizard turned toward Krusk and Gurn.

"It's their show, I guess," she said, jerking her thumb toward the half-orc and the azer.

The azer agreed. "Come here," he gestured toward Krusk.

All the companions moved toward the Opal Throne. With a

mild shock, Naull saw that it wasn't completely white after all. Along the back and sides were small, inscribed or enchanted circles of nearly translucent flame. Outside the city's protective aura, she suspected, those flames would burn without touching.

Each sigil appeared slightly different from every other, but they all looked at least a little like the key Krusk bore. When the half-orc drew it out the talisman blazed to life again, hovering slightly above his palm.

"Each of these circles once belonged to a lord of the Material Plane, or of Fire," the azer explained. "A lord could sit on the Opal Throne and open the conduits between the two planes, summoning forth spirits or beings of either, compelling them to serve by the same ancient compact that allowed us to build the city.

"The last lord of Secrustia Nar, corrupted by the perversions of the efreet, tried to command evil spirits of fire to invade the Material Plane, but we stopped him," the warden said, suddenly looking very old. He shook off the memory quickly, however, and continued, "We trapped his spirit in the Negative Energy Plane and he cannot be released while the city stands. All the lords surrendered their keys, except one." The azer pointed to the flame flickering in Krusk's meaty palm. "One was kept hidden, in case of disaster, in case we needed to open the gates again."

"Um . . ." Naull broke in when the azer paused. "I hate to interrupt, but why would you need to open them again? I mean, if no one was going to live here, then—"

"Some of the last lord's followers escaped," Gurn interrupted. The flames in his eyes were dark, like smoldering charcoal, and they matched the anger in his voice. "They followed dark gods and made evil bargains, and never gave up searching for a way to bring fire to the lands beyond the Elemental Planes. They sought ways to rescue the last lord of the city, too, but while the key remained hidden, that road remained barred."

"The blackguard . . ." Alhandra said, her voice full of dread.

The azer nodded in agreement and said, "Hextor, God of

Tyranny, Champion of Evil, Herald of Hell, and Scourge of Battle—he granted boons to those of the last lord's followers who worshiped him. They pledged themselves to the service of chaos in return for escaping our justice. Hextor always delights in cheating his brother of justice."

The fiery dwarf chuckled grimly and Naull looked from Gurn to Alhandra in alarm. The woman's white face was pale but she nodded once, sharply.

"Heironeous," she said.

The wizard saw the paladin's hand go to the emblem on her breastplate, the bolt of lightning in the grip of a strong fist.

"Heironeous," Gurn agreed, then he turned back to the throne, touching sigils quickly. "The war between gods spills onto mortals yet again. When you told me a blackguard was responsible for the burning of Kalpesh, the slaughter of the last Protector, and the pursuit of the key, I knew it would come to this."

"Do you know—" Regdar paused briefly—"her?"

The azer chuckled even as he worked. "No, no. At least, I hope not! No," he concluded at last, "but I know of her and her type. Blackguards rose in the city even as the last lord took power, and the worshipers of Hextor were chief among them. I am certain she is of the order of those who served the last lord and she has somehow gained knowledge of the key, and of the Opal Throne's power."

He turned his back on the heroes then, making a few more passes across the Opal Throne. Whatever ritual he performed was complicated, but Gurn continued talking.

"So now the key and the throne threaten our very existence. An evil creature who controlled the Opal Throne could command the forces of Fire, or release the dark one from his bonds."

Gurn finished and looked back at the companions somberly.

"It is time to return the key to the throne and shut the gate to the City of Fire forever."

He held out one brass-colored hand. Krusk slowly offered the glowing, hovering ball of fire to the azer.

But even as Krusk did so, Gurn started in surprise. Looking down, he saw an arrow protruding from his chest. Gazing up at the flickering walls of the tower, he pointed over the half-orc's shoulder.

Blasting through the flame came the black knight and two gnolls mounted on a flying carpet. The old gnoll had its bow in its hand and was already nocking another arrow. The younger gnoll leaped down off the carpet as soon as it passed through the flames, its axe in one hand and the vicious, hooked scimitar bare in the other. The gnoll leader howled its anger and hate as it charged.

"Look out!" Regdar shouted uselessly, pulling his sword from its sheath and trying to roll away from the swooping carpet, but he stumbled in his heavy armor and had to catch himself to keep from falling.

The old gnoll fired its second arrow at the azer, but Gurn dived behind the throne and the shaft broke against the wall. Krusk hesitated for a moment, then forced himself to toss the key under the throne. Sweeping out his axe, he returned the gnoll's war cry with a bellow of his own and sprang into battle.

Naull cursed as she fumbled with her new wand. Krusk was almost on top of the blackguard by the time she could aim and the explosion could crisp the half-orc along with the invaders if she spoke the command word. With her free hand she tried to find something in her component pouches that might prove useful, but she'd cast most of her best spells down in the cavern. The rest of her arsenal wouldn't prove more than a moment's annoyance to the blackguard.

Meanwhile, Regdar finished righting himself and Alhandra recovered from her surprise. The two followed Krusk into the fray. The older gnoll dropped its bow and leaped from the carpet just as Alhandra stabbed up at it with her sword. The blade tore the edge of the carpet but missed the gnoll. The humanoid drew its axe and circled around, trying to put the paladin between itself and its leader.

Regdar and the leader squared off near the white wall at the center of the room. The gnoll leader snarled and Regdar nearly growled himself. So intent was the fighter on the gnoll's two weapons that he failed to notice the black knight. After the older gnoll had jumped, she twisted the carpet around and leaped down lightly—amazingly lightly, considering her armor—behind the fighter. As the uncontrolled carpet fluttered down between the knight and Krusk, she moved to strike Regdar in the back.

Krusk bellowed, slashing with his greataxe around the fabric. He missed, but his shout of anger alerted Regdar and the fighter spun just in time to parry with his new sword. The two weapons rang and dark light from the blackguard's blade contrasted with the flaming walls. The black knight moved in to bind, and when the blades locked at the hilt, she pushed Regdar back toward the gnoll leader, laughing as she did so.

But Regdar refused to give much ground. He allowed the black knight to make him take one step back but just as it appeared he'd fall to the waiting gnoll leader's attack, Regdar pressed a small gem on the hilt of his bastard sword. The blade burst into flame and the blackguard sprang back, cursing. The flame singed her long hair but otherwise she appeared unhurt. One wave of the flaming brand made the gnoll spring away and Regdar turned back to the armored woman.

"I'll make you pay for that, filth!" she cried out in anger.

The old gnoll dueling with Alhandra was still hurting from the ambush, but it seemed to have a lifetime of dirty tricks to draw on. It feinted and circled, panting, trying to entice its fresher opponent into an unwary strike. Alhandra desperately wanted to dispatch this creature with the gray snout and help Regdar, but she let her training take over. She kept her impatience in check and did not charge as the gnoll expected. Indeed, the old gnoll took the paladin's hesitation for fear and its tongue lolled in anticipation. Springing forward suddenly, it brought its two-handed axe down in a smashing blow.

The attack was just what Alhandra was waiting for. At the last moment, she leaned to her right and let the axe hammer against her shield. Instead of an arm-jarring blow, however, the axe blade slid down the finely-worked metal and the gnoll stumbled. Alhandra slashed quickly at the humanaid's side. With a choking cry, the creature dropped its axe and fell to the floor. Dark blood poured out to spread in an almost invisible pool against the lava-colored floor. The paladin looked around for her true foe.

Seeing Kark fall beneath the paladin's blade, Grawltak felt a howl of grief rise in his throat, but he refused to let it out. He had the half-orc backed up against the Opal Throne and the barbarian's raging blows could not get past Grawltak's two weapons. As the half-orc surged forward again, Grawltak swept his hooked scimitar low and wide. The spike caught the half-orc just above the ankle. With a tug, Grawltak used the hook to trip him, then sprang back as the barbarian's awkward blow bit into the floor. The gnoll then hurled his hand axe at the half-orc and the missile sliced into the patchwork mail protecting the surprised barbarian's shoulder. The blade cut deep into gray flesh. Stepping forward, Grawltak stabbed at the barbarian who parried the blow with a wild swing and scrambled away.

Naull was the only one of the companions standing near the Opal Throne. She rushed to the azer's side and saw he'd already drawn the arrow from his chest and looked remarkably unhurt.

"Where is the key?" he asked.

Naull got on her hands and knees. She had seen Krusk toss it under the throne and it took only a few moments of blind fumbling for her to find it with her fingertips. The flickering flames made the disk hard for her to grasp, but the wizard managed to draw it toward her an inch at a time.

A howl of anger and pain distracted her. Looking up, Naull nearly screamed when she saw the blackguard, her face a mask of hate and triumph, standing over Regdar. He knelt before her, his flaming sword gripped loosely in one hand and his other arm wrapped around his belly. Blood flowed freely as he looked up at his foe. She raised her sword and laughed. When the fighter turned away from the blow, his eyes met Naull's.

"Regdar," Naull whispered in anguish.

His eyes held pain and despair but she saw something else there, too; something soft that they shared, but never had time to talk about.

Naull's right hand found a spell pouch and she pointed at the blackguard. She spat the command word and a thin, icy beam shot out and struck the black knight in her armored side. A small, white button of frost appeared on the woman's torso.

The blackguard didn't even notice. The sword came down.

Before the blow could land, before Naull could close her eyes, a gleaming shape streaked up from behind the blackguard. Silver arms wrapped around dark steel and both shapes crashed against the stone floor.

Alhandra had crossed the room in a flash, skirting past the gnoll leader and Krusk to tackle the blackguard from her blind side. They tumbled across the floor in a tangle of screeching metal.

The gnoll leader had seen the paladin dash by and tried to hook her with his curved blade, only to miss and curse its slowness. It cursed again for good measure when its mistress hit the floor. The gnoll stood momentarily alone, the only one in the room still on its feet, then it saw Naull lying beside the Opal Thone. Baring its teeth in a snarl of cruelty, the gnoll stepped toward the wizard.

If the gnoll leader saw Naull draw the red-tipped wand from her belt and point it just above its head, it showed no sign.

"*Secrus!*" she exclaimed, and the bead streaked out to a point barely above the gnoll's canine head.

When it exploded, the edge of the flame reached just short of Krusk and within inches of the bleeding Regdar, but its full fury engulfed the gnoll leader.

When the flames cleared moments later, only the gnoll's charred and crumbling corpse was left behind. Naull barely saw it as she struggled to her feet, so intent was she on reaching Regdar.

The wizard took one step, then two, then felt herself halt suddenly. It was as if something gripped her by the side. When Naull looked down, she wondered at the black steel jutting out from her midriff. Her eyes followed it to a hilt, and a black gauntlet, but pain clouded her vision before she could follow it farther. With a shudder, the wizard dropped her wand and heard it clatter against the blood-spattered floor.

"Well, that's about it, then," a voice said in her ear.

Naull struggled to turn her head and saw the blackguard's face only inches away. She fought to focus her mind and shut out the pain. In the throbbing haze, one corner of her mind noted how similar were this pale face framed with long, dark hair, and Alhandra's. Then her legs collapsed and she slid from the blade.

Lying on her side, Naull thought of Regdar and wondered if he still lived. She wondered, too, if the blackguard would place a foot on her chest as Alhandra had done to the gnoll in the street before delivering the final blow. Instead of feeling the black steel bite into her neck, however, she heard a clash of metal and a cry of pain. Turning her neck with a shudder, Naull saw Regdar swaying on his feet, his normally dark face pale from loss of blood. He staggered toward the black-armored woman, his flaming sword trailing sparks along the floor. Behind him, Alhandra struggled forward on one knee, hand outstretched. She seemed to be trying to say something, but when she opened her mouth, only blood sputtered forth.

The blackguard turned back from the grisly pair and looked down at Naull again.

"Give me that," she said coldly.

At first, the wizard didn't understand, then she looked at her hand that was pinned under her body and saw the fiery key hovering above it. She didn't know how it did that; perhaps its magic had been activated when she touched it beneath the throne. Either way, the blackguard wanted it, and for some reason she was waiting for Naull to give it to her.

The wizard didn't move at first, then the blackguard crouched down, reaching toward Naull's bloodstreaked hand.

With a desperate effort, Naull pushed away. She was surprised at the strength still in her arms. The pain in her midsection flared like icy blades and her body left a bloody smear on the floor where she passed. It hurt even more to use her legs, but dragging herself with only her arms was so slow. With despair she realized that she was only behind the throne, bare yards from where she started.

The blackguard's ebony gauntlet gripped her shoulder and Naull cried out weakly in shock. As the hand tugged her back, Naull gritted her teeth and threw the key away from her as far as she could.

It wasn't much of a throw. The key bounced and skittered like a flaming coal jumping out of a fireplace and came to rest about a dozen feet away. Naull heard the blackguard curse and felt the metal gauntlet smash against her ear.

"Fool!" the raven-haired woman spat in annoyance.

Standing over the fallen wizard she looked at the key and at the bleeding woman. Victory was in her grasp. Naull saw the blade glint above her face. Weakly she pawed at her spell pouches. She thought of Trebba spending her last breath to stab the orc lieutenant and desperately hoped she could find something that might save her companions.

The wizard's probing fingers found the small black bead taken from the orc lair. Naull hadn't fully identified it yet, but when she discerned its magical nature she knew it was an evocation spell of some sort. Now it was her only hope. She drew it out and threw it up at the blackguard and the raised sword.

The black bead struck the knight's armor with a small *tink!* For a brief instant, neither Naull nor the blackguard thought it would have any effect. Then with a roar of displaced air, the space around the two exploded.

Alhandra stumbled over to Regdar and the two lurched forward. Regdar collapsed just feet from the edge of the explosion and coughed blood. Reaching out with a mailed fist, he felt it stop against an invisible field of force.

Naull lay inside a bubble of force. Regdar couldn't tell whether she was alive or dead, but he saw her wound and kept trying to touch her. The force wall stopped him, and he sagged against it.

A warm lightness swelled up against his back and Regdar felt himself regaining some of his strength. He blinked and spat out blood. Turning, he saw Alhandra with blood on her chin as well. She was concentrating gravely as she put her hands on his back, and Regdar felt his wound healing.

She stopped almost immediately and while Regdar knew he was still hurt, he also knew he would live. Alhandra staggered to her feet and looked around. When she saw Krusk lying to one side with the azer tending his wound, she walked slowly toward him.

Regdar turned back to Naull.

A sword clashed against the force wall just as he put his hand up against it. Reflexively, the fighter jumped to his feet.

Inside the bubble of force stood the blackguard, the symbol of Hextor emblazoned in red upon her dark armor. She looked a little worse for wear, her face dark from bruises and her hair singed and tangled. She screamed angrily at Regdar and pounded futilely against the bubble. Regdar ignored her and looked down.

Naull lay at the blackguard's feet. He thought she was

unconscious—he even hoped she was unconscious—but then she turned her face toward him and he almost looked away. Her features were scorched and bloody and one eye looked as if it might be damaged beyond normal healing. She reached up and put her hand against the bubble.

"Naull..." Regdar said, pressing his hand to the wall near hers.

The wizard coughed bubbles of blood.

"Got her..." she said, and smiled grotesquely.

The blackguard cursed but they both ignored her.

"Are you...?" Regdar didn't complete the question. "How did you...?" He gestured.

"Bead of force," she answered feebly. "Figured it had to be something. Didn't think it would be this good." She smiled weakly, then coughed again and said, "Get the key."

Regdar didn't move. Alhandra stood behind him, however, looking a little better. She felt her way around the invisible bubble to the flaming key. The paladin picked it up and brought it back, then showed it to Naull, who smiled again.

The blackguard's eyes lit up. She brandished her sword and pointed its dark tip at Naull's chest. The wizard didn't react.

"That's it, little sister," the blackguard taunted, holding the sword in one hand and beckoning with the other. "Give me the key, and I will spare your friend. I can heal her, you know."

Alhandra hesitated.

"Can she?" Regdar asked. His voice sounded hollow.

The paladin looked at Naull, then the floor, then back at Regdar, and said, "Not like I do. If she ever served a power of light, Hextor has perverted her ability. He grants the power to destroy, not to heal others."

Alhandra locked gazes with the blackguard.

"Oh?" The blackguard sneered. She tossed her head back and laughed cruelly. Pulling out a short, stoppered bottle, she dangled it in front of the paladin. "Even a servant of Hextor can pour a potion down a girl's throat."

"Alhandra—" Regdar said, pleading.

The paladin nodded, defeated. She held up the key and they watched as a smile grew on the blackguard's face.

"No," coughed Naull, spitting more blood. Regdar saw that she was weakening quickly. Whatever was keeping her conscious was killing her as well. "No, Regdar, you mustn't. She'll kill us all. You don't have much time."

Krusk and the azer joined them. The half-orc pressed his hand against the bubble and tears rolled down his gray cheeks. Naull looked up at him and tried to smile but the pain was too great. She only grimaced.

Gurn said solemnly, "She is correct. I have prepared the throne, but the ritual is fading. If we do not complete it and place the key in its spot, we cannot try again for at least another day."

"Naull," Regdar started to say, but she shook her head. Her eyes were open and clear. Refusing to look away from his partner, Regdar nodded. "All right. Do it."

Ignoring the blackguard's threats and curses, Alhandra handed the key to Krusk and Gurn told the half-orc to sit in the chair.

"Put your right hand here and hold the key with your left," he said.

Alhandra and Regdar stayed at the edge of the bubble. Regdar knelt there, his hand covering Naull's and his eyes shining with grief. The expression exchanged between Alhandra and the black-guard was pure hatred.

"I will kill you for this, little sister," the blackguard spat at her. "I have marked you, paladin of Heironeous, and I will find you again. As Hextor has sworn eternal hatred for his loathsome brother, I swear my hatred for you!"

"Likewise," the paladin replied coolly.

Naull looked to be unconscious, but she still breathed shallowly. Regdar said her name quietly as the azer and Krusk began the last element of the ritual. The blackguard turned away from Alhandra and looked down at the pair, contempt plain on her features.

"As for her . . ." the black knight purred.

Regdar looked up at her sharply. His eyes met the blackguard's and she looked amused at his rage.

"This bubble won't hold me forever, and I'll have her for company in the meantime."

Regdar stood and brandished his sword. If he was about to make a threat, however, Gurn interrupted it. "Now!" the azer yelled, and Regdar turned just in time to see Krusk slam the flaming key against the Opal Throne.

The entire tower bucked. Alhandra barely kept her feet and Regdar didn't, falling back against the bubble of force, then landing heavily on the stone floor. He peered into the bubble trying to see Naull's face again but the quake turned her body away from his.

Scrambling to his feet he shouted, "What's happening?"

Krusk stood up from the throne as Gurn answered, "The gates are being closed and the city will return to fire. Secrustia Nar is no more."

Gurn looked both sad and relieved when he said this, but Regdar reacted with alarm.

"What about them?"

He turned back to the bubble as the ground shook again. A crack appeared in the white wall and he felt the temperature rapidly rising.

"No time!" Alhandra shouted. "We have to leave!"

With an anguished look back at the bubble, Regdar let Krusk drag him away. The blackguard, rather than looking afraid for her life or even angry that her scheme was thwarted, looked at him with that same smile of taunting satisfaction she'd shown moments before. She knelt by Naull's side and said something, but Regdar couldn't hear over the thunder around him.

"Listen!" the azer said. The harshness of Gurn's voice jarred Regdar out of his reverie and he looked at the fiery dwarf. "My mephit servants—they should be able to get you back to the street, but then you must run for the gate. There isn't much time.

I'm sorry for your friend; I did not think the collapse would happen so quickly."

Regdar wanted to argue, but another rumble interrupted him. More cracks appeared in the white wall and the floors. A mephit, followed by a dozen more, swirled up around him. He felt himself lifted off the ground then he landed heavily again. He swatted at the azer's servants and growled.

"Come on," Alhandra pleaded with the fighter.

Regdar saw the creatures of smoke and fire try to lift her as well. She did not resist, but they had trouble anyway.

"Your armor," the azer said. "It may be too heavy."

"No!" Krusk said suddenly. "Here!"

He threw something heavy at their feet.

It was the blackguard's carpet, torn and singed, but when Alhandra stepped cautiously aboard it rippled to life.

"Come on," she yelled again, reaching out to Regdar. The fighter turned back toward the bubble but Alhandra grabbed him. Lurching with surprise, Regdar stumbled onto the carpet, then tried again to pull away. A thick forearm wrapped around his neck from behind and squeezed, harder than anything Regdar had ever felt. He struggled with all his might without catching a wisp of breath. He twisted and kicked, but still felt himself being dragged inexorably backward onto the carpet. Regdar's eyes locked on Naull's body as darkness crept in from the edges of his vision. The carpet rose with Krusk cradling the fighter's unconscious body between his knees, rocking back and forth.

Standing on the shifting lava floor, the azer watched as the paladin steered the carpet through the minaret's swirling flame walls and out over the crumbling city.

Outside the tower, pieces of the building were breaking loose and falling away. The flaming walls flickered and blazed in surges of heat. This did not trouble Gurn. He did not fear the flames and he fingered a small ring that he knew would keep him from falling.

Moving around the throne to the bubble of force, the azer looked at the blackguard. She no longer smiled, but looked off into the sky at her departing enemies.

The azer moved around to face the blackguard.

"You have failed," he said simply.

She shrugged. "This time, slave, this time. Hextor hoped to gain a servant from my mission, and I hoped to gain powerful magic." Looking down at Naull's unconscious form she concluded, "perhaps all is not lost."

"You are," Gurn pronounced. More of the floor collapsed, beginning a long plummet to the burning city below. The bubble of force teetered near the edge of the broken tower. "I will see you burn, servant of Hextor. Secrustia Nar may be destroyed, but it will never serve evil again. And neither will you."

The blackguard laughed. She laughed as the fires erupted around the azer's feet and he glared at her and thought her mad. Before the rest of the tower could fall into the fire, however, she stopped laughing. Drawing an amulet from beneath her breastplate, she looked at it and placed it on the ground. A moment later, she chanted words in an ancient and foul language. A blue form rose from the disk and spoke to the blackguard in the same language. Nodding, the black knight knelt and picked up the disk and the body of the wizard.

The azer's eyes narrowed, but he could do nothing. With a last, jaunty wave, the blackguard, the wizard, and the disk winked away. Moments later, the tower groaned, twisted visibly, and toppled lengthwise. Gurn hovered above it and watched its long, graceful fall into the roiling flames. With a last look at the inferno that had been the white tower, the azer sighed and turned away.

Epilogue… Regdar, Krusk, and Alhandra stood at the base of the canyon as the sun set over the edge. Alhandra's lantern provided some light, but after their travels through Secrustia Nar it seemed feeble indeed.

While waiting for Regdar to regain consciousness, Alhandra and Krusk had searched the canyon for their horses. As Alhandra feared, the gnolls had found them, but while Stalker died a bloody death, Windlass had fled to safety. The beast returned at Alhandra's calls, and Krusk marveled aloud at the horse's training.

"Some day," Alhandra said in answer to the half-orc's questions, "if I am true to my calling and serve Heironeous faithfully, he may give me a mount to use in his service. Until then," she said, tossing Windlass's mane and smiling slightly, "my pretty lass will have to do."

Regdar hung his head as Alhandra watered and tended her horse. He'd woken badly, at the cave mouth above the canyon, and nearly fallen off. When the initial shock and anger wore off, he forgave Krusk for choking him unconscious. He hadn't spoken to Alhandra.

When the paladin finished with her mount, Krusk was off trying to find something for them to eat. Their packs were left behind in the City of Fire and they had only one waterskin between them.

"I'm sorry," Alhandra said finally.

Regdar didn't respond immediately. When Krusk found his way back to them, clutching a pair of dead lizards in his fist, the fighter spoke.

"It's all right, Alhandra," he said heavily. "It's all right."

The paladin put her hand out to reassure him, but Regdar leaned away. She let her hand fall as if the slight meant nothing.

"What are you going to do now?" Regdar asked. He sounded almost casual, but Alhandra heard the tightness in his voice.

"I talked it over with Krusk while you were recovering," Alhandra said. "We're going to Kalpesh. If—" Alhandra paused for a moment, then continued in an even voice— "her army is still there, maybe we can do something about it. If Kalpesh is destroyed . . ." She shrugged. "Krusk needs to know, and maybe we can help the survivors. Who knows?" she added hopefully, "maybe the army disintegrated when the blackguard left."

"Maybe," Regdar said, looking back up at the cave.

"I don't know that we could have done anything differently, Regdar," Alhandra said.

She wished there had been something else to do, but she'd been overmatched. The blackguard of Hextor threw her around like a rag doll. Only Naull's sacrifice allowed the rest of them to escape.

"We could have been better," Regdar answered bitterly. "We could have planned better, or fought better, or damn-well killed her instead of letting Naull—" The fighter broke off.

"Sacrifice herself," Krusk said. The other two looked at the half-orc with a little surprise. He met each of their stares with his own mismatched gaze in turn. "She knew she had to do something important. She died doing it, so we could live," he said, staring at Regdar. He turned his gaze back to Alhandra. "So we could continue fighting."

"At least Naull took the blackguard with her," Alhandra added to Krusk's unusual insight.

"At least," Regdar said hollowly, but he agreed with Krusk. "And we will get better."

Straightening his gear and checking his bandage, Regdar looked ready to go.

"What about food?" Krusk asked. He held up the dead lizards.

A ghost of a smile came over the fighter's face and he said, "You two enjoy. Two lizards isn't much to share across three plates." He stepped out northward. "I might be able to reach Durandell before my stomach thinks those little beasties look edible."

Krusk put on a slightly injured look, then laughed. He held out a meaty hand and Regdar accepted it in his mailed grip. The barbarian patted Regdar's armored shoulder.

"You're welcome to come with us," Alhandra said, and Krusk nodded almost eagerly.

"You fight good," he added.

Regdar thought for a moment but shook his head. "No. I'm going back to Durandell. I want to see how they made out, and check on Ian. Maybe he can help me find out where the gnolls and the blackguard came from." His voice seemed light, but his eyes were hard.

"It's a long walk back," Alhandra said, "and we're going the other way."

"I'll make it," Regdar answered. He clutched his side as he started off. "Eventually. At least I won't have to eat Krusk's cooking."

"Here," Alhandra said, tossing him a big, rolled bundle. Regdar caught it with an expression of surprise. It was the flying carpet. "Windlass won't fit on it."

He looked up at the half-orc, who shrugged.

"Don't like heights," he said, sounding a little embarrassed.

The three laughed as the last rays of the sun lost themselves over the cliff face.

The War of Souls

The sweeping saga from best-selling authors
Margaret Weis & Tracy Hickman

The stunning climax to the epic trilogy!
Dragons of a Vanished Moon
Volume III

War and destruction wrack the elven homelands as Mina
marches on the last stronghold of the Solamnic Knights.
Driven to desperation, a small band of heroes allies with
a Dragon Overlord to challenge once and for all the
mysterious One God. And through it all, a kender named
Tasslehoff holds the key to the past—and future—of Krynn.

The New York Times bestseller
now available in paperback!
Dragons of a Lost Star
Volume II

The charismatic young warrior-woman Mina leads a loyal army
on a march of death across Ansalon. Against the dark tide stands
a strange group of heroes: a tortured Knight, an agonized mage,
an ageless cleric, and a small, lighthearted kender. On their
shoulders rests the fate of the world.

Sembia

The perfect entry point into
the richly detailed world of the
FORGOTTEN REALMS®, this
ground-breaking series continues
with these all-new novels.

HEIRS OF PROPHECY

By Lisa Smedman

The maid Larajin has more secrets in her life than she ever
bargained for, but when an unknown evil fuels a war between
Sembia and the elves of the Tangled Trees, secrets pile on secrets
and threaten to bury her once and for all.

SANDS OF THE SOUL

By Voronica Whitney-Robinson

Tazi has never felt so alone. Unable to trust anyone, frightened
of her enemy's malign power, and knowing that it was more
luck than skill that saved her the last time, she comes to realize
that the consequences of the necromancer's plans could shake
the foundations of her world.

November 2002